Catch Me:
Brie's Submission #3

By
Red Phoenix

Catch Me: Brie's Submission

Copyright © 2016 by Red Phoenix
Print Edition

RedPhoenix69@live.com

Edited by Amy Parker, Proofed by Marilyn Cooper
Cover by CopperLynn
Phoenix symbol by Nicole Delfs

*Previously published as part of *Brie Learns the Art of Submission*
Adult Reading Material (18+)

Dedication

I would not only like to give a shout-out to MrRed, but to our three (four) children.
They have been supportive of my journey as an author, going so far as to help me in the publishing process and even attending fan parties.
My kids are everything to me,
and I couldn't be prouder or love them more.

As always, I want to thank my fans as well.
You spoil me with your friendship!

CONTENTS

A Total MF 1

Ineptitude 15

Mind Over Matter 33

Serving her Khan 43

Preparing for Graduation 58

The Interviews Begin 66

It Gets Complicated 82

Brie Bows Before *Him* 109

Her First Lesson 122

Lesson Two: The Heart 134

Misguided Service 143

Lesson Three: A Matter of Ego 151

A Little Restraint 166

The Wolf Returns 172

Repentance 186

Visiting the Center 193

Lea and the Subs 207

His Electric Touch 217

The Haven 224

Toasted Brie 234

A Desperate Move...241

Thane..254

Other Red Phoenix Books 265

Connect with Red on Substance B 269

A Total MF

B rie stopped at the entrance to Mr. Gallant's class-room. She hesitated for a second before dutifully untying her corset, but he stopped her. "Miss Bennett, that is unnecessary. I am your teacher. The ritual is only meant for your trainers."

She quickly retied it, feeling embarrassed by her mistake, but that changed as soon as he gestured her to a chair with a smile. She sat down directly in front of his desk. It was strange being the only student in class, and she had to shake off the loneliness.

Mr. Gallant began, "Normally, I would hand you an evaluation by your Dom from the previous Auction Day. However, our time tonight is extremely short. In a nutshell, Mr. Wallace noticed that you struggled with his authority early on, but stated the problem resolved itself. He rated you a ten overall."

Brie hid her smile. *A ten, huh?*

Her tiny but commanding teacher then got up from his desk and handed Brie a different packet. "You will be filling out the same questionnaire you completed when you enrolled in the course. Take time to answer the questions thoroughly. It will help us to structure this last week more effectively."

Brie took the packet, feeling discouraged. It would take forever to fill out. Mr. Gallant then went back to his desk and opened a drawer, then pulled out Brie's fantasy journal. A smile spread across her face when he placed it on the edge of her desk.

"After you are done with the questionnaire, I would like you to write down your last fantasy for us. Something a little more edgy, this time."

Brie's eyes widened at the prospect. Writing in her fantasy journal was always a treat, but the way Mr. Gallant had made it sound, the journal entry for this week was going to be used in a scene. She went to open the journal up, but he stopped her. "No journaling until the packet is complete."

Ah, the carrot…

She dutifully opened to the first page of the packet and began filling out the numerous questions. Instead of being a chore, it was fascinating. She had changed a lot as a person in a short amount of time. Brie giggled when she came across the part where she had to rate different BSDM activities. She remembered marking anal sex and caning as two things she had not wanted to try. This time around, she marked both 'Like'. Less than six weeks ago, she had been scared of African American men, due to her traumatic experiences as a child in public school, but Baron had managed to change that. Fear of the unknown also had no power over her. She now embraced and *wanted* to experience the unknown. Four years in college hadn't produced the kind of results her six-week course had.

When Brie finished, she looked up and asked, "Mr. Gallant, can I ask you a personal question?"

He looked up from his book and replied, "You can ask, but I don't guarantee I will answer."

"Are you a Dominant?"

"Yes."

I knew it! "May I ask another question?"

"Same rule applies."

"Understood." Brie couldn't help blushing when she spoke. "Why don't you have training sessions with the students?"

Mr. Gallant put his fingertips together in a thoughtful pose, considering his reply before answering her. "I don't normally share my personal life, Miss Bennett. However, I will as long as you keep it between us." When she nodded, he continued, "I have a monogamous relationship with my submissive, who also happens to be my wife."

His answer melted Brie's heart. "Thank you, Mr. Gallant."

"I take it you are finished with the packet."

She held it up and smiled. "I am. It was quite eye-opening, to say the least. I've changed a lot."

He returned her smile. "I quite agree, Miss Bennett. Please hand it to me and start on your journal." He looked at the clock and added, "You only have twenty minutes. Use the time wisely."

Brie grinned at his little reminder. Too many times, she had gotten too caught up in the backstory to fully describe her fantasy. That was *not* going to happen tonight.

She opened the luxurious book. Mr. Gallant had had them record many delightful fantasies onto those beautiful gold-lined pages over the past six weeks. Fantasies she would be able to share with her Master... The burglar and the helpless housewife. The pirate and the virgin. The big, bad wolf and Little Red Riding Hood. The sheik and the slave girl. And now she was about to add another—one with a little more bite. She picked up her special journaling pen and began to pour out her thoughts. She kept the backstory painfully short, not wanting to chance running out of time.

Backstory—16th century King, innocent daughter of a destitute royal.

****

I am frightened. I know I have been sent to the King as a peace offering. This is my father's desperate attempt to stave off the creditors. If the King accepts me, my family will continue to live at the manor. If not, we will be left homeless with no title and no means of support.

I pinch my cheeks one more time, hoping he will find the blush on my cream complexion appealing. I am escorted before the King, who is busy devouring a lavish meal. My stomach growls and a real blush creeps over my face.

My stately King looks up from his plate. "Is this the one?"

"She is, Sire."

"Looks a little too young and untried. Not what I want tonight. Take her away."

I blurt out, "I may be untried, my Lord, but I am willing."

He gives me a second glance. "Willing? What does that really

mean coming from a little girl? You know not what you propose."
He motions me away, but I am determined.

"I am yours, my Lord, to use as you please." I bow before him
in complete supplication.

"I will not be gentle or kind," he warns.

"Let me please you, my King."

He snorts in amusement. "So be it." He points to the old
servant holding the flask of wine beside him. "Pleasure him with
your mouth while I watch."

My heart beats fiercely as I approach the servant. I have never
given oral pleasures before and have no idea how to go about it. My
King takes the wine flask from the stunned man and laughs as he
sets it down on the table. "Been a long time, has it, Thomas?"

"Yes, Sire."

"Good. Then this shouldn't take long." My King looks at me
and says drolly, "Go on, girl. Please your King."

I fumble at untying the man's trousers and I hear my King
chuckle unkindly. I pull down his pants, along with his undergar-
ments, and am shocked at the largeness of his staff. I've never seen
one before and find it intimidating.

"Go on, child," my King commands, pushing me down on my
knees before the old servant.

I open my mouth hesitantly and stick out my tongue, licking
the end of his member. It twitches and I back away. I can hear the
dissatisfied grunt of my King and quickly recover from my shock. I
lick it again and a bitter taste fills my mouth. I do not retreat.
Instead, I lick it more eagerly.

"Take him in your mouth."

With my heart pounding, I open my lips and the old man's
shaft fills my mouth. My cry is muffled when he pushes himself in
deeper.

"That's it. Suck his staff with that virginal mouth until he comes."

The old man grabs my head and starts thrusting his member harder and harder. I know my King is watching so I moan, holding the thick member with one hand. Suddenly, the rigid member begins pulsing in my mouth. The old man groans loudly as copious amounts of bitter fluid burst forth from his manhood.

"Swallow it all," my King commands.

I swallow without question, distressed when some of the liquid escapes my lips. The servant pulls his shaft from my mouth with a satisfied sigh. I wipe the extra from my mouth, but my King growls, "I said swallow it all."

I lick my hands, making sure to clean off all of the bitter liquid.

My King sits back in his chair and smiles wickedly at me. "That was entertaining, but I am not convinced you are worthy."

While Thomas pulls up his trousers, I bow to my King. "How may I prove myself, Lord?"

"I assume you are a virgin."

"Yes, my King." I am completely prepared to sacrifice my virginity to my sovereign.

But he surprises me when he says, "You shall give your maidenhood to my priest. That would entertain me on so many levels."

I gasp at his audaciousness, but dutifully answer, "It would be my pleasure, my Lord."

He snaps his fingers. "Get young Father Christopher. Tell him… Tell him I have a special assignment only my priest can perform."

I watch with frightened curiosity as the soldiers leave to retrieve the priest…

"Miss Bennett."

Brie looked up from her journal and pouted.

"Don't tell me—you're just getting to the good part."

She sighed. "Well, yes…" Unfortunately, her imagination was too prolific.

"As in the past, I am sure the Dom will be able to work with what you've written."

Her curiosity was killing her, so she asked, "Mr. Gallant, since we aren't having another auction, who will be playing out our fantasies?"

He stood up and took the journal from her. "It is a standing tradition that your last entry is used as a training exercise."

Brie squelched a smile, wondering if she would be seeing Greg again, the first Dom she had ever been partnered with. He would make an excellent Thomas. But who would play the part of the priest? The possibilities were fun to entertain.

"You will proceed to room five, where Master Coen is waiting for you."

She got up to leave and was almost out of the door when she spontaneously turned around. "Mr. Gallant?"

"Yes, Miss Bennett."

"You are an extraordinary teacher. Thank you for everything." She scooted out of the room, afraid she might cry if she stayed. She hated to think of not sitting in his class next week.

As she walked down the hall, she saw Lea entering room nine. She gave her friend an enthusiastic wave and smiled when Lea waved back before disappearing into the room. Brie's six-inch heels clicked pleasantly down the hallway. It was good to be a submissive.

Brie was curious what Master Coen had in store for her when she opened the door and noticed a fire going in a small brazier next to a thin wooden table in the middle of the room.

She stopped at the door and untied her corset, then laid it on the floor before kneeling in front of Master Coen, her arms behind her back to display her breasts in the pose assigned to her as part of her ritual. She kept her head bowed until he came to her and placed his hand on her head. "You may serve me. Stand."

Brie gracefully got to her feet and faced him, intrigued by the fire. She had a hard time not staring at it.

"This is the last week of training. We have a rite for all graduating submissives. It is not a requirement, but it speaks volumes to your dedication."

That fire suddenly looked far more sinister. "I understand, Master Coen."

He picked up an iron rod from the fire. "Do you know what this is?"

She shook her head, although she was certain what it was.

"This is a branding iron, Miss Bennett. Our school emblem will be branded on your inner right thigh. Think of it as our seal of approval."

Brie's eyes widened in terror. The idea of having her flesh burned in the most sensitive of places was horrifying.

"Rest assured, we take this seriously and will use the safest measures. Your health is not in danger; however, I will not perform the branding without your approval as it is a permanent mark."

Brie looked at the bright red end of the branding iron. The school crest looked to be about a square inch and a half. Not huge, but it would be noticeable if she wore a bikini. She swallowed hard. Was she willing to be marked like this? She closed her eyes to focus and had a long conversation with herself.

Brie finally came to the conclusion that she was proud to be a graduate of the Submissive Training Center. There were so few in the world that it made her exceptional and worthy of a tattoo—even if it was in the form of a branding. "I'll do it."

She noticed a gleam in Master Coen's eye at her choice. "Very well. Remove all your clothing and lie on the table while I ready things."

She watched him thrust the iron back into the coals. She shuddered, but started to undress. It seemed surreal, but he was busy taking out rubbing alcohol and rubber gloves. Then he rolled up his sleeves in preparation.

This is really happening...

When she was naked, she went to the table and put her hands on it as support. She hesitated before getting onto the hard, unforgiving piece of furniture. *You can do this, Brie.*

Master Coen said nothing as he watched. He was extremely patient, apparently understanding how difficult this was for her. She finally pushed herself onto the table and lay down. "Put the soles of your feet together," he ordered.

She did, and it naturally spread her thighs out, giving him easy access. He put on the rubber gloves and soaked a cotton ball with rubbing alcohol. He spread it liberally over her right inner thigh. The coolness of the liquid made her nipples tighten into hard nubs—of course, her fear also helped. Brie looked up at the ceiling and commanded herself to breathe slowly. *Thank goodness for Tono's training.*

"We need to let the alcohol dry fully and allow the iron to heat up," he commented.

She bit her lip and sighed.

"You are in good company, Miss Bennett. In the world there are less than five hundred submissives who wear this mark."

Brie nodded. If almost five hundred women had survived this, she would too. "Master Coen, could you explain the crest? I want to know what I am being branded with."

"Certainly. The two letter symbols are Alpha and Omega. The Alpha stands over the Omega. The collar represents submission and the heart-shaped lock is a reminder it is given in love. The words are Respect, Obey, Submit."

"I like that," she said.

"Good, as it will be burned into your skin."

Master Coen was *not* helping. Brie remained silent, psyching herself up for the fearsome ordeal. But she was distracted as Master Coen began binding her feet, and then her thighs, moving up to her wrists last. "It is imperative that I prevent any movement."

He picked up a blindfold. "This will make it easier. In the past it was done without, but submissives find it helpful."

Brie willingly lifted her head and let him cover her eyes. Suddenly it felt more real. She was bound and blind, waiting for the brand to burn into her skin. Part of her wanted to scream out the safe word, but she knew she would not. She was in it to the end—fear would not win over her determination.

"I am marking your skin so that I get it in the right spot." Her loins contracted in horror as a marker glided over her skin in a circular pattern. She bit on her lip harder, concentrating on the pain rather than what was about to occur.

"I must ask a final time. Do you want to be branded?"

'Want' is not the right word. 'Willing but terrified' is more like it. She nodded.

"No, I must hear words."

Brie's voice trembled. "I want the branding."

"It shall be done."

She heard him messing with items on the table and then the sound of the iron rod as he hit it against the edge of the metal brazier, presumably to knock the ashes off. "When I am about to apply the brand, I will tell you to breathe out. Take a deep breath now and hold it."

Brie inhaled deeply and held it in. Her rapidly beating heart protested, wanting her to let it out. She felt the heat of the brand next to her skin. Dangerously close and blistering hot.

"Breathe out."

She let out the breath just as the intense heat seared her. She heard the sound of her sizzling skin and screamed, almost blacking out. Master Coen removed the brand and put it back in the fire. "How do you feel, Miss Bennett?"

She didn't hold back the tears. "It hurts!"

"Would you like to see it?"

She nodded and felt him untying the blindfold. Master Coen helped her sit up. Brie took a deep breath before she looked.

The creamy skin of her right thigh was unmarked. She shook her head and looked at the left one. There was nothing on either. She looked up at Master Coen questioningly.

"The power of the mind."

When he untied her wrists, Brie hesitantly caressed the skin of her thigh, not quite believing she hadn't been branded because she could still feel the aftereffects of it on her skin.

"It felt so real."

"The power of suggestion, Miss Bennett, is quite potent. I told you what was about to happen; your mind accepted it and responded accordingly."

"But I felt the hot iron and heard my skin burning."

"I switched the heat of the brand with the chill of ice and I sprinkled water into the fire. Effective alternatives to trick the senses."

Brie lay back down, still feeling dazed. "That's crazy."

"This exercise demonstrates the intense power of suggestion."

She chuckled nervously. "You're not kidding!"

Brie shuddered; the reality that she hadn't been branded not quite registering. Master Coen smiled down at her as he undid her bindings. "You were brave, Miss Bennett. Quite impressive."

She frowned and turned from him. "Not so impressive when nothing happened. I feel like an idiot."

He picked her up in his large, muscular arms and carried her to a lounge chair in the corner, holding her like a child. "You do not appreciate it yet, but you are a prime candidate for mind play. Your creative nature makes you a charming plaything."

She looked at him sadly. "That sounds like a bad quality to me."

"On the contrary, in the hands of a trusted Dom the possibilities are limitless."

A shuddering sigh escaped her lips, remnants of the emotional experience. Master Coen held her tighter. "We are going to explore erotic hypnosis with you this week. After today's session, I believe you will be successful and will appreciate the experience."

She tentatively touched his square jaw with her fingertips. "Master Coen, the idea both excites *and* frightens me."

"I understand. However, erotic hypnosis is not meant to be a mind-fuck."

"Mind-fuck?"

"What you just experienced. Being led to believe something for the amusement of the Dominant. Erotic hypnosis is mutually enjoyable and will enhance your ability to explore sexual experiences you could not before."

Master Coen reached between her legs and began lightly stroking her clit. Brie closed her eyes and relaxed under his attention. "I have seen few submissives with your courage or stubbornness."

She opened her eyes and gave him a tentative smile. "Thank you?"

He chuckled. "Yes, it was meant as a compliment. Lie still and accept your reward for that gutsy display."

His fingers began flicking at a quicker pace, causing a slow burn in her pelvis. Brie tilted her head back and moaned. He met her lips with his own. His kiss was gentle, in stark contrast to his burly exterior. It appeared Master Coen had a softer side, one that she was just now beginning to see. It didn't take long before her hips were bucking against his hand in pleasurable release. It felt so intimate, so sweet to come in his arms like that.

"Thank you, Master," she whispered.

He kissed her forehead. "I take pleasure in rewarding my subs. Just ask the two I have at home."

She could just imagine his harem of girls, waiting to service Master Coen's every need. A threesome might work for some, but Brie wanted exclusive rights to her Dom.

"Tomorrow you will be working with Master Anderson after a short session with Marquis Gray in room forty-two. They will be providing you with lessons based on your interest in becoming a full-time sub. However…" He laughed aloud. "I doubt it's what you are expecting."

He refused to elaborate, which made Brie excruciatingly curious. She had never been on that side of the school and couldn't begin to imagine what was hidden in those rooms.

Ineptitude

When Brie pulled up to the school the following night, she was overwhelmed by disappointment. Blue Eyes was still missing. She hadn't been overly concerned on Monday when he hadn't been at the door, but two days in a row seemed odd for him. Brie wondered if it was a rule that they couldn't fraternize after an auction, or if Faelan was training extra hard now that his class was also coming to a close. *Our last week...* The thought depressed her.

She hurried to classroom forty-two, anxious to discover what unusual encounter Marquis had planned for her. Brie swung open the door and stopped cold. It was a kitchen.

Marquis stood beside the counter, along with Mary and Lea. "Running behind, Miss Bennett?"

She glanced up at the clock. Still five minutes early, but that seemed to mean nothing at this school. "Sorry, Marquis Gray." She dutifully untied her corset, then set it to the side before kneeling in front of him. He ignored her, speaking to the other two girls instead.

"If you wish to be a full-time submissive, it will be expected that you can cook. You have heard the way to a man's heart is through his stomach? Well, in your case, the way to a Dom's good graces is through pleasing his discerning palate."

Brie's jaw dropped. *Cooking?* That was one area she had no talent for or interest in. She desperately wanted to question him on it, but would not be allowed to until he acknowledged her.

"Although we are only going to touch on the basics today, you should be able to produce a few exceptional dishes to please a variety of tastes. I shall start you off. Once you prove you have mastered this basic skill, you will move onto Master Anderson in room forty-eight. He is trained as a gourmet chef and will further your education."

Marquis Gray walked over to Brie and placed his hand on her head. "Come join us, pearl, but re-dress. I do not want to see burns on those lovely breasts."

Brie nodded, smiling inside. Marquis knew just how to tweak her ego.

There were five stoves in the large room. He directed her to the one closest to Lea's. "You three will cook omelets for me."

Mary raised her hand. "What if I don't know how?"

"Do your best. I want to see the extent of your cooking knowledge."

Brie groaned inside. This was not going to be pretty...

There was already a pan on the stove and a bunch of ingredients set in bowls. At least they had made it easy for her. Brie cracked a couple of eggs into the skillet and fished out the shells. She threw in a pat of butter and turned the stove on high. She remembered something about needing to sear the outside. While she waited, she sprinkled a little bacon, lots of cheese, and a touch of parsley for color. When the eggs started bubbling, she grabbed the spatula and attempted to turn it. The omelet would not come off the pan. She scraped the bottom, and noticed it was a little too brown. She took it off the burner and finished scraping the egg from the pan. It was a hot, scrambled mess.

"Please present your omelet attractively on the plate and give it to me," Marquis instructed.

Brie looked over at Lea, who tilted her pan and let her omelet slip out onto the plate. At a little flick of her wrist before it was completely out, it folded neatly in two. Lea put a sprig of parsley and a thin wedge of twisted orange slice on the side for decoration. It was disgusting how easy she'd made it look!

Brie patted her brown scrambled eggs into the shape of an omelet and handed it to Marquis with her head bowed in shame. She took a quick glance at Mary's plate and was relieved to see that hers was not much better.

All three girls stood before him as he tasted their work. He started with Lea's first. "Nice color. Pleasing to the eye." He cut off just the end and took a bite. After chewing it for a few seconds, he swallowed. "Good consistency; appropriate seasoning; nice ingredient choice. I really cannot help you further, Ms. Taylor. You may proceed to Master Anderson."

Brie wanted to protest. She had been looking forward to spending time with her best friend. Instead, she had to watch Lea collect her thong at the door, slip it on and bow to Marquis before leaving.

Marquis Gray went for Mary's next. He had a hard time cutting through it with his fork and did not look anxious to place the bite in his mouth. He chewed it for much longer than he had Lea's and swallowed hard. "Rubbery. Way too much salt." He addressed Mary directly. "Did I ask you for an omelet, Miss Wilson?"

"Yes, Marquis Gray."

"Then why did you give me a fried egg?"

"I… Isn't it an omelet?"

He pushed the plate away. "No. It is not."

Brie trembled when he took her plate. He shook his head when he tried to cut it and it just fell apart. He looked hesitant as he put the forkful in his mouth, then spat the egg back onto the plate.

"Horribly burnt, inedible and no seasoning to speak of. What were you thinking, Miss Bennett?"

She burned with humiliation when she admitted, "I can't cook."

"Obviously, but have you never been in a kitchen?"

She stared at her feet when she answered, "My mom did all the cooking. I just kind of watched."

"Did you learn *nothing*?"

It clawed at Brie's insides to know she was a complete failure. She'd never thought for one second her cooking skills would play into her role as a submissive.

He walked over to the stove Lea had previously occupied. "I will instruct you both on how to make a decent omelet. Pay attention. I will not repeat myself."

Mary looked over at Brie and shrugged. At least the two of them were in it together.

"First, you should get your pan heating on medium heat. To get a fluffy consistency, I separate the egg whites and whip them." He was quick and precise as he cracked and separated three eggs. "Add a tablespoon of water and whip until it is incorporated. Then whip the egg yolks in a separate bowl, add a little salt and pepper to taste and fold the egg whites in gently."

He showed the girls how to scoop from the bottom and fold it over the top of the whites. "Don't over-fold or you will eliminate the air pockets you just created." He put it down and put two pats of butter in the pan. "Take it off the heat while the butter melts. Once it is completely melted, you can put it back on. This prevents you burning the butter—a common mistake."

He put the pan back on and poured the mixture into it. "Add your favorite ingredients. I personally like a touch of green onion and bacon. Wait until it starts to set and then swirl the pan around to cook the run-off, like so." He swirled the runny eggs so that they met the side of the pan. "When they look almost done, sprinkle with cheese. Aged Gouda and Swiss cheese are my preferences. Once it is melted, you can plate."

Marquis held up a dish and tilted the pan so the eggs slid out. Just like Lea, he did a little flip of the pan so that the omelet folded into a perfect half-moon. Brie was tempted to clap, it looked so pretty.

"I want you both to taste it. Specifically notice the texture, the seasoning, and the look of the cooked eggs. I expect you to duplicate it."

Both girls took a fork and cut into his omelet. It was like cutting into a moist piece of cake. Brie took a bite and moaned in pleasure. Man, if she could cook like this her Dom would be kissing her feet…just before he commanded that she kneel and flogged her for a job well done.

"Begin."

Brie gave Mary a wink. Now that she knew what she was doing, she would be out of here in no time. She followed his example of separating eggs, but went to dig out the shells.

"Throw it out. I will not eat shells," Marquis snapped.

She poured them out and started again. After several tries, she had a shell-less concoction. She put the butter in and watched it melt. When she saw the butter turn brown, she realized she'd forgotten to take the pan off the heat.

"Start again."

Brie sighed. Mary was already handing Marquis her second omelet. Brie held her breath while he tasted it. "Still rubber. Try again." *Looks like we're cut from the same cloth, Mary.*

The two continued through trial and error to replicate Marquis' fluffy omelet. Brie could not get the hang of the wrist flip at the end and her omelets looked funky, but she was definitely improving—or so she thought.

Ten omelets later, Marquis snorted in disgust when they presented him with their attempts. "No!" He pushed the plate back to Brie. "Look, does that look golden or brown? Don't even bother serving it. There is nothing more disgusting than burnt eggs."

Brie went back to start a new one. She sighed at Mary when a shell fell in. She dumped the eggs and started again.

"There. That is close to the original. Do it again so that I know it's not just a fluke."

Brie watched in dismay as Mary started on her final omelet. She didn't want to be the last one in the room.

Nothing about cooking came naturally to Brie. It was a mystery and even with instructions there was still a finesse she lacked, but she wasn't going to let it stop her. Brie sprinkled the ingredients in and started twirling the pan. Too soon. She put it down and waited for the eggs to start bubbling. She kept glancing over at Mary, who suddenly seemed to know what she was doing.

The distraction caused Brie to brown the eggs and she had to throw the finished omelet away. She started afresh, groaning as Mary handed Marquis Gray her completed dish. He took a large forkful and chewed on it for several seconds. A smile spread across his face. "Acceptable. You may join Ms. Taylor in room forty-eight."

Mary winked at Brie on the way out.

Oh, crap.

"Miss Bennett, now that Miss Wilson isn't here to distract you, I trust you will succeed in cooking a simple egg dish."

"Yes, Marquis Gray."

Having all of the attention on her proved to be more pressure than she could handle. Marquis had to send out for more eggs. "Even if it takes all night, Miss Bennett, you will cook me the perfect omelet."

Brie's frustration grew as she failed omelet after omelet. It was painfully obvious cooking was not in her nature and she wanted to give up. However, Marquis would not hear of it. He was a formidable taskmaster, brutally honest and uncompromising. When she handed him her twenty-first attempt and he took a bite, he growled, "I will kill Thane for electing me for this assignment."

It turned out that twenty-four was the magic number. "Although I am going to vomit, this is a good omelet." He sighed and added, "Now make another."

Brie wanted to cry with relief. She hurried to make another masterpiece. Three omelets later, he finally gave his seal of approval.

Marquis Gray looked up at the clock and shook his head. "You only have twenty-five minutes until your practicum." He frowned and then stood up. "Unfortunately, there's nothing else to be done," he mumbled, as if to himself. Then, to Brie, he added, "Here, let me show you an easy pasta dish no one can decimate... Not even you."

He collected premade noodles from the refrigerator and made a quick Italian dish consisting of freshly cut tomatoes, garlic, fresh basil and olive oil. Despite the simplicity of the ingredients, it was delectable— restaurant quality. The challenge for Brie was not making the tomato sauce, it was getting the noodles al dente. With just a few minutes to spare, Brie was able to present him with a satisfactory dish.

"You truly fail as a cook, Miss Bennett. In all my

years of training I have never seen such ineptitude. I insist that you sign up for cooking lessons after this course."

Brie bowed before him, mortified beyond belief, but she was grateful to be leaving the kitchen. "Thank you, Marquis Gray."

"Leave. I must find a bucket to relieve myself of your cooking."

"Where do I go, Master?"

He shook his head. "You are not allowed to call me Master after this." He chuckled afterwards, so she figured he was joking. "Meet Master Anderson in room forty-eight."

Brie's heart sank. *More cooking?* "Beg your pardon, Marquis Gray, but I thought my practicum was starting."

He looked at her thoughtfully. "It is. You are spending the evening with Master Anderson. You will be joining him at the party he is hosting. Thank heavens the other two girls proved better cooks, or he would have nothing to serve."

Brie made her way to Master Anderson. Her back tingled in remembrance of his masterful skill with the bullwhip. She wondered what to expect at the party. Would she be scrubbing toilets next?

She was surprised and disappointed that the other two girls were not in the room with the talented trainer. "Good evening, Miss Bennett."

She remembered the ritual and readied to undress, but he told her, "There's no time. Come bow before me." She came over to him and offered the homage he was due. His deep voice reverberated in her loins. "You are a lovely thing. Stand up and serve your Master."

She was grateful he didn't comment on where she had been for the last two hours. Brie helped Master Anderson load up boxes of prepared food, then followed him to his car.

"Do you understand what will be asked of you tonight, Miss Bennett?"

"No, Master Anderson."

On the drive to his place, he explained, "You will act as the gracious hostess. See to my guests' food and beverage needs. Smile and move gracefully throughout the rooms as you care for my special guests. I want every eye on you. I want them to envy me for the beauty only I control."

The way Master Anderson talked made her long to please him. "It will be my honor, Master Anderson."

"Tonight I would prefer you to simply call me Master, young Brie."

She thought it was funny that Marquis had forbidden her from using that title a short time earlier. "Yes, Master."

When they got to his home, an old Victorian, he directed her to his bedroom. "Your clothes are laid out for you. Dress and return to me."

Brie hurried to the door he'd pointed out. It was definitely a masculine bedroom, with a dark brown color scheme, a leather lounger, and sports equipment on the wall. If his decor was any indication, the man was heavily into rowing and archery.

He had chosen a formfitting black dress for her, along with fishnet hose and five-inch heels. She appreciated his thoughtfulness concerning the heels. She gratefully exchanged six-inch for five and sought out her Dom for the evening.

"Ah, my beauty. Come to your Master."

Brie walked up to him and was taken by surprise when he grabbed her ass and pressed her against his waist. His massive arousal was easy to detect beneath his business suit. "I remember your courage, young Brie. It stirs your Master to think of it."

She wanted to service his need and asked, "How may I please you, Master?"

His smile was devastating, almost heart-stopping. "As we still have a bit before guests arrive, I believe now is a good time to show you my Room. I have a much nicer set-up in my other home..."

He walked her down a narrow hallway and unlocked the door at the end, then ushered her inside. It was illuminated by a soft, candle-like glow. She was immediately drawn to the wall of extensive BDSM toys and equipment, including his infamous bullwhip.

"Lie on the table so that I may play with you."

"Do you want me to disrobe, Master?"

"Only the dress and panties."

He went over to his wall and scanned his equipment, apparently looking for something in particular while she removed the clothes and lay down for him.

"Ah, there it is..."

Master Anderson approached Brie, holding a black hood. She felt a bit queasy as he gently placed it over her head and secured it around her neck. It took away a sense of self to have the hood cover her face, and she didn't like it.

"First time with a hood?" he asked, although it sounded as if he already knew her answer.

She nodded, feeling mute under the black sheath.

"It will heighten different senses. Don't you feel it?"

She realized he was right. Her sense of touch was magnified because of her sight and sense of smell being taken away. Even her sense of hearing was affected as she listened to herself breathe inside the hood.

She felt a light, prickling sensation run up her inner thigh. Goose bumps took over the area. She heard his light chuckle. "You must be new to the Wartenberg Wheel as well. It is a charming tool. I can lightly tickle or bring prickling pain." She stiffened at his words, but he responded by caressing her thigh with his warm hand. "I do not cause pain needlessly, young Brie. Every tool, every action is gauged to bring the most pleasure. Tonight, I tease your body as I acquaint you with something new."

Brie relaxed and gave in to the sensation. He ran the spur-like wheel over her exposed skin, acclimating her to its unique pleasure. Once he had her skin tingling from it, she heard his belt buckle being undone.

She was surprised to feel his shaft press against her pussy and immediately reacted. "I can't!" Brie tried to scoot backwards, but he held her still. She cried out from inside the hood, "I can only couple with my trainer if other trainers are around, Master."

He chuckled lightly as his tight grip on her loosened. "Ah, but I am not technically a staff member of the Center. The rules do not apply to me, young Brie."

She nodded her head inside the hood and relaxed back on the table.

"Do not worry, I wouldn't risk your training or my reputation," he said soothingly as he began caressing her pussy with his massive cock. He spread her legs wider, coating his manhood with her juices as he readied Brie for penetration.

When he finally pushed the head of his large shaft inside her, she found herself grunting from effort. She'd forgotten just how big Master Anderson was and had to force her body to relax to a greater degree. Master was a challenging man to receive.

"So tight," he exclaimed appreciatively as he pushed himself in deeper.

Brie could just imagine his immense manhood opening her up. The vision of it turned her on and she tilted her hips to further his progress.

"Good…" he growled hoarsely. Master Anderson began thrusting his dick into her, causing Brie to cry out. There was nothing like being filled past capacity to make a girl lose herself. Her senses blurred as Master Anderson fucked her with his mammoth cock. It pulled and tugged her into another reality. Soon she felt him shudder inside her warm depths.

It gave Brie an intoxicating sense of power. Not only could she take his manly shaft in its entirety, but she could bring him nirvana.

Master Anderson quickly disengaged and removed the hood. "The favor shall be returned later, but for now we must receive our guests."

He helped her with her dress and teased her hair to

maintain the just-fucked look. Then he cleaned his instrument before returning it to the wall.

He turned to her and grinned enchantingly. "Let the fun begin."

The two walked into the foyer just in time to receive the first of his many guests. Brie about dropped to her knees when she opened the door to Mr. Holloway, the producer of two of the most popular cable series on TV. Her big chance stood before her, and all she could do was stare at him like a complete idiot.

Master Anderson came up behind her, placing his hand on the small of her back while holding out the other to give the producer's a hearty shake. "I am glad you could make it, Mr. Holloway. I know Miss Bennett is grateful to make your acquaintance as well."

"Ah, yes, Miss Bennett. The table trick."

Brie blanched at his remark.

He seemed to find amusement in her discomfort and smiled. "So Gray didn't tell you I was the designated lookout in case you failed in your task to be discreet."

To hide her shock, she shook her head good-naturedly and asked, "May I take your coat, Mr. Holloway?"

He shrugged off his jacket and handed it to her, then dug into his shirt pocket and pulled out a card. "Gray says you are filming a documentary about the Center. I should have some time off in three months. Give me a call then and I'll give it a look."

Brie took the card and answered in a calm voice, "I will be sure to do that, thank you." Thank heavens for her sub training! It saved her from falling all over him and making a fool of herself.

Within an hour, the house was full to capacity and Brie was running around serving drinks, along with exotic finger foods prepared by her two friends. She was floating on cloud nine. Mr. Holloway knew who she was and wanted to look at her documentary! Her break had finally come and it was all due to Marquis Gray, the man she'd nearly poisoned with her cooking earlier. She kissed the card and grinned to herself.

Brie suspected there were several submissives in attendance based on their postures and attentiveness to their 'dates'. It became obvious when she walked into the study to care for her guests and found a submissive bent over an armchair, receiving a hard pounding. Seeing it so unexpectedly was both a shock and a turn-on.

The participants ignored her, so she quietly left the room and headed to the large entertainment area, where she was treated to another copulation scene. This time it was a young man taking a dick deep in the ass from a skinny but lusty Latino.

Master Anderson walked over to Brie, ignoring the erotic scene. "I have a friend I would like you to meet." He guided her over to a scenic window where an Australian she'd served earlier was waiting. He was of Aboriginal ancestry, with a wide face and beautiful dark skin. His accent had delighted her when she'd heard it earlier but he was extremely quiet, so she asked a question in order to get him to speak. "What may I serve you?"

Master Anderson answered for him. "Actually, young Brie, the item he seeks is you."

She was suddenly reminded of Rytsar's party. However, this time her Master wanted to 'share'. She glanced over at the young sub and saw the Latino had brought out a paddle. A party devoted to sub play... What a concept.

Brie turned to Master Anderson. She was open to the experience, so she bowed low at his feet. "What is your pleasure, Master?"

"That's my beauty. Present yourself to us," her Master commanded.

She immediately dropped to the floor before the men, her head down and her legs as open as her little black dress would allow. She felt them both caress her as they slowly removed her clothing. The Aborigine had a soft touch, light like a feather. It intrigued Brie, and she began to focus on his subtle caresses because of the delirious way they made her feel.

She felt Master Anderson leave her side, but was distracted when her other partner began nibbling on her hip bone. It was light and ticklish, making her twist and writhe underneath him. His laughter had a lilting quality she found charming. He continued to tease her until Master Anderson returned.

She saw he had a set of nipple clamps in his hand, connected by a delicate chain. She bit her lip, feeling her loins close up. Clamping her nipples had never been enjoyable. It was simply something to endure for her Dom's pleasure.

"Not a fan of the clamps?" Master Anderson asked.

She snuck a peek at him. "No, Master."

"Shall I change that?"

Brie doubted he had that kind of power, but she appreciated his offer. "Please, Master."

She watched as he unscrewed the alligator clamps. He turned to her other partner and said, "Cobar, would you do the honors?"

Cobar's dark hands moved to her nipples, and he began pinching and tugging on them ever so lightly. Because she was already sensitized to his unique touch, her nipples hardened instantaneously.

"I see you have a way with her," Master Anderson commented. "Very good." He placed the device on her nipple and clamped it shut. It barely squeezed her nipple because it was so loose. Then he began tightening the screw. "Let me know when it starts to feel uncomfortable."

Brie nodded and soon voiced her discomfort. He turned it one more full rotation and she squeaked. "It will start to feel better in a few seconds." He moved to the other nipple and used the same technique. Brie's nipples throbbed, but not in an unbearable way like they had in the past, and she felt the heat rush to her pussy. Master Anderson truly was a talented Dom. No wonder Sir respected him so much.

"And now for the pièce de résistance." He put the chain in her mouth. "Pull on it to your comfort level. Up and side to side."

Brie did as he asked and felt her nipples tug in the direction of her mouth. It was erotic to have that kind of control over her own nipple stimulation. She experimented with how much tension she could handle, completely forgetting about the men until Master

Anderson spoke.

"I never tire of that, Cobar. I don't believe there is anything more exquisite than a woman pleasuring herself."

"Although it is beautiful, Brad, there is something I enjoy more." Her new partner moved between her legs and started fingering her pussy, taking light licks of her clit. Brie moaned against the chain.

"Somehow, I'm not surprised…" Master Anderson murmured as he leaned over and began sucking on her neck.

Oh, my God, I am in sub heaven, Brie thought.

Mind Over Matter

A fter such an erotic party, Brie had struggled to fall asleep. She'd never guessed what hotness lay behind Master Anderson's reserved manner. That Dom was a submissive's dream—if that sub wasn't already torn between four men. Brie chose not to dwell on her decision. She trusted Sir's assertion that comparing Dominants side by side would make it evident who was her true Master. Besides, Brie wasn't about to let her indecision ruin her last few days of training.

She was surprised the next evening when she entered the room for her practicum. Lea was already there, kneeling in her ritual pose, waiting for acknowledgement. Brie quickly stripped off her corset and knelt beside her. Even though they couldn't speak to one another, it was exciting to be in class together.

Mary showed up a minute later and bowed at the threshold of the door.

Sir's smooth voice flowed over Brie. "Before you begin your practicums tonight, we have a longstanding tradition at this school." He stood up and walked over to

Lea first. "Stand before the panel, Lea Taylor."

Lea stood up, but kept her head bowed.

He walked to Brie next and touched her on the shoulder. She trembled under his hand and wondered if he could feel it. "Brianna Bennett, stand before the panel."

She rocked back on her heels and stood up. His proximity felt like the disturbance in the air before a lightning strike.

He walked over to Mary last. "Mary Wilson, come forward and stand before the panel."

Mary moved up beside Brie. The three submissives were now in a straight line in front of the panel. It felt like old times again.

Master Coen spoke to the students. "You are coming to the end of your training at the Center. As a reward for your dedication, one of your trainers will fulfill the last entry in your journal."

Brie stopped breathing. *Please don't let it be Ms. Clark!*

Marquis Gray stood up with their fantasy journals. He walked over and handed them out to each of the girls. "You will pick a name at random. The trainer selected is your partner for the scene. You will then hand over your journal." He sat back down before adding, "Expect to hear from your chosen trainer tomorrow before class begins."

Ms. Clark got up next and walked over to the girls, holding a red velvet bag in her hand. She addressed Lea first—naturally. "Pick a name, Ms. Taylor."

Lea stuck her hand in and swirled it around a few times before choosing. She pulled out a piece of paper, which Ms. Clark took from her. The Domme opened it up and announced, "Master Anderson."

Lea obediently walked over to the trainer and handed over her book. Brie couldn't help noticing the blush that colored both Lea's cheeks and her chest. *Must be happy about getting Master of the Bullwhip as her partner.*

Ms. Clark skipped over Brie and went to Mary next. Mary dug into the bag and unceremoniously handed her choice over to Ms. Clark. "Master Coen," the trainer stated.

Mary dutifully handed her journal to the muscled trainer. Knowing of her friend's hots for the guy, Brie suspected she was pleased, but Mary didn't show it.

Ms. Clark then turned to Brie. Only three names remained: Sir, Marquis, and...Ms. Clark. Brie tentatively put her hand into the bag, as if it were full of poisonous snakes. As soon as her fingers landed on a piece of paper she grasped it. She was certain it was the Domme's name, but her fingers wouldn't let it go. Brie slowly drew it out and handed it over with an inward groan. She watched Ms. Clark's face as the trainer opened it and was disheartened when her eyes narrowed.

Double crap!

The Domme frowned when she announced, "Sir Thane Davis."

Brie wobbled a little, not quite believing it.

"Don't just stand there. Hand the journal over, Miss Bennett," she barked.

On feet that seemed not to touch the ground, Brie glided over to Sir and gave him her precious fantasy journal. His face was devoid of emotion as he took it from her. Brie did not miss the look of reservation on Marquis' face and understood that Sir would have to tread lightly.

As she walked back to the girls, she gave them a huge victory grin. *A whole night alone with Sir!* She could just die.

Her joy was soon tempered, however. After Ms. Clark sat down, Sir addressed the girls. "Tonight you will each be working with one of the trainers in an area requiring specific expertise. Based on your recent questionnaires, as well as our observations over the last six weeks, we feel tonight's exposure will benefit you. If the experience proves to be more than you can handle, you are free to use your safe words. Keep in mind that you are in the hands of experts. We would not jeopardize your health or well-being." His warning sent prickles down Brie's back.

"Miss Wilson, you have expressed an interest in blood play. Marquis Gray is well versed in the practice, so you will join him in room nineteen."

"Thank you, Sir," Mary said, her voice hinting at her obvious excitement.

"Miss Bennett, you will be joining Ms. Clark to experience erotic hypnosis in room thirty."

Brie wanted to cry out for mercy, but she bowed her head and said, "Thank you, Sir." If enduring Ms. Clark was the price she must pay to be with Sir, so be it.

"Ms. Taylor, you have shown interest in fisting. Master Coen has extensive experience with the practice. You will join him in room two."

"Oh, thank you, Sir!"

Brie shuddered. What was Lea thinking? That girl was into all kinds of kink.

"Miss Bennett and Ms. Taylor, you may re-dress before you follow your trainers out. Miss Wilson, you are free to leave with Marquis Gray."

Mary looked positively radiant as she followed Marquis out the door. Lea quickly slipped on her thong and practically skipped behind Master Coen. Brie took her time as she retied her corset. Ms. Clark was not in the mood to wait and came over. She tied it far tighter than Brie was used to. The trainer looked her over and said, "Now you look enchanting."

Brie had to slow her breathing to endure the tightness of the corset. Although the tighter look appealed to Ms. Clark, it made serious demands on Brie's body. It reminded her of Tono's binding, but was not nearly as sexy.

She left the safety of the panel to follow the Domme to their designated room. Brie had images of being made to cluck like a chicken. She thoroughly expected to be humiliated by the woman, but at least she had the safe word. Tonight, of all nights, she was grateful for that power.

Their heels echoed through the hallway together. There was something sexy about the sound of it. Ms. Clark opened the door to a room which contained a bed, a table set with candles, and a single red satin chair.

"Undress except for the corset and lie on the bed."

Her Mistress went to a panel on the wall, and suddenly the air was filled with soft music. She lit the candles before she turned down the lights. Mistress looked approvingly at Brie and said, "Your body looks charming in candlelight."

Two compliments within minutes of each other? It didn't seem natural, but Ms. Clark sounded sincere. "Thank you, Mistress."

Mistress removed her jacket and shirt sensually, then she unzipped her tight business skirt and shimmied it to the floor. Ms. Clark certainly had a knack for stripping. She stood before Brie in a red bra and thong, with black garter belt and hose accenting her long shapely legs. Brie found herself thinking again, *If I had a thing for women, I think I would be in love.*

"Close your eyes and let me touch you. Listen to my words, but do not feel the need to focus. Let go and relax…"

At first, Brie felt stupid. Her Domme lightly brushed her hands over Brie's skin, but she couldn't stop herself from twitching when Mistress grazed her mound.

"Let my fingers help you to unwind."

Brie took a deep breath and forced her muscles to relax. She put herself in the mind of a submissive. This wasn't about her—it was about giving in to the experience Mistress was creating. It was okay if her body enjoyed the stimulation.

"That's better… Listen to my voice and relax for your Mistress. Let the tension drip from your fingertips to the floor."

Brie lay there willingly in the hands of her Domme. The woman had a way with her delicate but sure touch, to which Brie's body responded. It wasn't long before she was floating on a blanket of calm.

Mistress laid a weighted blindfold over her eyes. It served not only to blind, but also to lightly hold her head in place. Surprisingly, it was comforting and Brie felt another layer of resistance fall away.

"Do you smell the candles?" Mistress asked.

"Yes, they smell of vanilla."

"Odd. They are jasmine."

Brie could just pick up the slightest hint of jasmine.

"Jasmine aids in opening all your senses. Concentrate on the smell and let it unlock your mental boundaries."

Brie was unsure if Mistress was playing a trick on her, but when she inhaled again, she definitely detected the distinct aroma and drew it into her body.

"Have you ever orgasmed to palm stimulation?"

Brie would have shaken her head because she was feeling so relaxed, but the blindfold prevented it so she answered verbally. "No, Mistress."

"Spread your legs apart slightly so that your clit is exposed to the air." Mistress helped her to position her legs and cooed soothingly, "A lovely cunny...one that deserves to climax."

Hearing those erotic words come from Ms. Clark's lips helped Brie to understand Lea's crush on the woman. Whether the trainer was faking it or not, Brie's pussy appreciated her suggestion and was beginning to feel the heat.

Mistress took Brie's right hand and turned it palm side up. She lightly traced her fingernails over the contours of the sub's hand. It sent shivers throughout Brie's entire body.

Ms. Clark said soothingly, "As I stimulate your palm

you will begin to feel an ever-increasing temperature rise in your loins. I want you to resist it. I do not want you to come until I give you permission. Do you understand?"

"Yes, Mistress."

She began making concentric circles in Brie's palm. Every time she reached the middle, the burning in Brie's groin intensified. "Resist it," Mistress reminded her gently.

Brie's palm tingled with an electrical current that traveled up her arm and into her core. When Mistress took her hand away for a second, Brie's pussy began to throb. She gasped when the fingertip returned and continued its sensual stimulation.

"Is your pussy wet?"

"Yes, Mistress."

"Is your pussy eager?"

Brie moaned, "Yes, Mistress."

"Do you feel that burn deep inside?"

Brie's inner muscles contracted lightly in response. "Yes, Mistress."

"Concentrate on your nipples. Are they tightening in anticipation?"

Brie felt her nipples push against the corset as they squeezed into hard buds. Her body was primed and ready for the sexless orgasm.

Mistress stopped what she was doing and brought Brie's hand to her lips. Brie felt the lightest breath of warm, moist air on her skin and whimpered.

"This time, I am going to count down from five. When I reach one, you will come."

Brie's breathing came in short gasps. Mistress gently

laid Brie's hand on her lap and started slowly circling the inside of her palm. "Five…four…three…" Brie thighs squeezed together of their own accord. "Two…" The chill washed over her. "One…"

Brie cried out as her pussy started pulsating. Her orgasm was subtle, but it was definitely a real orgasm.

"Good sub." Mistress patted her palm before standing up. Brie waited several minutes before Ms. Clark took off the blindfold. Brie noticed she was fully dressed.

"What did you think, Miss Bennett?"

Brie suddenly understood how Ms. Clark must have felt when Brie had made her orgasm through cunnilingus. It was weird to have experienced pleasure at the hands of an unwanted partner. But the experience itself had been amazing. To come without any stimulation to her pussy had been extraordinary and she was grateful for the experience.

"I liked it very much, Mistress."

"Call me by my trainer title."

The scene was officially over. "Yes, Ms. Clark."

"I'm glad to hear you enjoyed it. Dress—we have a short stop before you can leave."

Brie quickly dressed, keeping her eyes to the floor as she followed Ms. Clark out of the room. They walked back down the hallway straight to Sir's office.

Ms. Clark knocked on the frame of the door. "We are done."

Sir looked up from his desk. "How did it go?"

"I found her quite easy to manipulate, quite easy indeed. I consider our Miss Bennett to be a hypnosis slut."

And the old Ms. Clark returns…

Sir turned his attention to Brie. "Miss Bennett, what did you think of the experience?"

Despite Ms. Clark's insult, she smiled into Sir's gorgeous eyes. "It was amazing, Sir."

He nodded to her in a fatherly way. "Excellent. You are dismissed. Expect my call in the morning." He looked at Ms. Clark. "Please stay behind. I would like to talk with you."

Brie couldn't wait to spend time with Sir without prying eyes, and would have skipped down the hallway if her shoes had allowed it.

Serving her Khan

B rie received a text message at precisely eight o'clock
the next morning: *Dress in clothes provided. Prepare
your body for your Dom. I will come by to pick you up at 6 PM.*

She couldn't even think straight after that. Spending
a whole night with Sir was unimaginable! She fumbled
her way through work. Mr. Reynolds was startled when
her drawer came up fifteen dollars short.

"What's going on, Brie? This is so unlike you."

As embarrassing as it was, she didn't really care. She
would be in Sir's arms tonight. "Mr. Reynolds, can I just
pay you the fifteen dollars?"

"That's not how it works, Brie. I have to write you
up, per store policy."

She smiled. "Okay. Do whatever you have to."

Mr. Reynolds shook his head. "What's happened?"

Brie giggled and blurted, "I have a hot date tonight!"

He frowned, but she could tell it was forced. "A hot
date is not an excuse for a short drawer."

"Honest, I will try to keep more focused tomorrow,
but I feel too wonderful to care right now."

"I think you should stay home tomorrow," he stated.

"No, Mr. Reynolds, I'm sorry! You know this isn't normal for me."

"It would be best if you don't come in tomorrow. Understand I will send you home if you show up."

Brie felt horrible. "Mr. Reynolds…"

"Think of it as a vacation. Of course, it is an unpaid vacation, but you can sleep in tomorrow morning."

She gave him a quick hug and left with a skip in her step. Tonight she would be under the domination of Sir…

Brie came home to find a large package at her front door. She excitedly picked it up and took it into her tiny apartment. Surprises were a weakness of hers, so she ripped into it before shutting the door. When she'd lifted off the lid and pulled back the tissue paper, she gasped in delight. Not only was there a sequined gown of gold and black, but there were also classy six-inch heels, a black lace garter belt, silk hose, and a sexy front-clasp bra and panty set. His taste was impeccable.

Brie purred when she lifted up the dress, noting the sleek gold zipper down the front, and held it against her. She danced in a circle, imagining how the night would play out. How would Sir take her kingly fantasy and make it a reality? It was obvious he would be going with a modern scene. Would he end up playing the priest? She desperately hoped so!

She took extra time shaving, caressing her skin with oils, manicuring her nails, and styling her hair. She wanted to be perfect for Sir. Then she waited anxiously by the door, willing the doorbell to ring.

Exactly at six, he came for her. She straightened her dress and smoothed out her hair one last time before opening the door to him. She couldn't breathe when she saw the man standing before her. Sir was dressed in a striking suit of dark gray. His brown hair was brushed back loosely and he wore a naughty smirk—the kind that turned Brie into putty. Over his arm, he carried a fur.

She held onto the doorknob for support. "Good evening, Sir."

"Tonight you will call me Khan." So he was playing the role of a ruler. What did that mean for the evening—for her?

"If it pleases you, Khan."

"Turn around for me, girl."

Brie turned slowly for him, basking in his rapt attention. He shut the door before he exclaimed, "This will not do."

Sir put down the fur wrap and grabbed the hem of her dress, pulling at the seams. She heard them rip.

"Better."

Brie looked back and saw that the slit of her dress nearly reached the crease of her ass now. He caressed her buttocks before peeling off the black lace panties. He threw them in the box. "It was a mistake to include these. Totally unnecessary." The authoritative way he handled her was sexy and already had her moist between the legs. "Face the wall."

She turned away from him and purred when he took her wrists and tied them together behind her back. Was he going to ravish her now?

Instead of being taken by Sir, she felt the fur caress

her shoulders as it covered her arms from view. "My elegant property," he murmured in her ear. He placed his arm on her back and guided her out of the apartment.

Brie felt the butterflies start as he led her to a limousine. The driver opened the door and Sir helped her into the vehicle. The oversized seats were made of leather and it looked as if the limo could hold at least twelve people.

Sir sat down beside her and nodded to the driver before he shut the door. Sir grasped her chin and kissed her roughly. Brie's heart did a flip-flop.

"You are here for my pleasure," he stated, setting up the fantasy.

"Yes, Khan."

"You will not deny me."

"No, Khan."

She expected him to take her then, but he buckled her in the seat and moved across from her. He sat with his legs open in a relaxed but powerful position. Sir spent the drive staring at her, saying nothing.

When they arrived, Brie expected to see an upscale restaurant but was greeted by the sight of a warehouse instead. Sir guided his shocked submissive over the cracking asphalt and into the building. The expansive warehouse housed an arena. The place was smoky and crowded with men, making it difficult to see the main entertainment, a large metal cage in the middle of the building. Inside the enclosure two men, both bloody and beaten, fought ruthlessly as the crowd cheered on. Brie shuddered and turned away as one of the men took a solid kick to the head and crashed to the floor.

"Watch your victor, girl," Sir told her.

Brie watched in dismay as the downed man was repeatedly beaten until the referee finally called the fight. The crowd went wild as the champion raised his fist in the air. He exited the cage and was accosted by fans as he made his way through the multitudes. The fighter was stopped by Sir's driver. After a brief conversation, the muscle-bound man turned and headed straight towards Brie. He looked fierce with his large muscles and tattoo-covered chest.

She held her breath, wondering what Sir had in mind. The wild-eyed man approached her, obviously high from the fight. A smile spread across his face as he looked her over. "My prize?"

"Yes," Sir said as he removed the fur and untied Brie's wrists. "Pleasure your victor with your mouth, girl."

Ah, Thomas... But a much sexier version compared to her fantasy.

She knelt on the cement in her beautiful dress before the fearsome fighter. The man jerked down his shorts, exposing a throbbing, hard cock. She hesitantly grasped his shaft, in keeping with her virgin persona, and tentatively licked the head of his manhood in front of the now hushed crowd.

Brie inhaled his musky scent, getting off on the manly aroma. She lightly fluttered her tongue across his frenulum and felt his body stiffen. Then she took his meaty shaft into her mouth. He grabbed the back of her head and pushed her farther onto his cock. Luckily, Brie was experienced enough to take his enthusiastic handling. She whimpered softly on his manhood, lightly caressing his balls with her hand.

He wasn't satisfied with a blow job, however, and pushed her onto all fours, hiking up her dress. She fully expected to feel his shaft ram into her, but Sir heaved him off her. "No!"

Sir helped Brie off the ground, straightening her dress and brushing off her knees before he turned to the stunned fighter. "Never take more than you are offered."

Brie stood there quietly as he placed the fur back over her shoulders and walked her out. He murmured in her ear as they were leaving, "Although that proved entertaining, I am not sure you are worthy yet." He nodded to a young male selling tickets at the entrance. The gossamer blond with an angelic face immediately handed over the tickets and cash to another employee and followed them out.

Brie's heart was racing. The boy had to be her 'priest'.

Sir escorted her back to the limousine and helped her inside. The boy was directed to the back to watch while Sir sat beside Brie. He looked her over critically, as if he were still deciding her merit. "If I do not find you pleasing, the evening will end."

She swallowed hard, unsure if he was acting or if he actually meant it. "I long to please you, Khan."

"Lie down, girl. Let me examine your feminine wares."

Brie lay down on the leather seat that stretched the length of the limo. Sir moved closer and slowly ran his hand up her leg. She tried to look into his eyes, but he was focused on watching his hand move up her thigh. He lifted the hem, exposing her bare mound. She felt a rush of heat as he stared at her lustfully. "A fine flower, ripe for the picking."

His hands went to the zipper between her breasts. With deliberate precision, he pulled it down one link at a time. His agonizing slowness made the reveal that much more exciting. When he finally pulled the material aside, Brie gasped. Her chest rose and fell rapidly as he caressed her lace-covered breasts and trailed his fingers down her stomach.

"You are beautiful, girl, but are you appropriately responsive?" Sir's hand moved between her legs and petted her sex. Brie bit her lip and resisted the urge to press against his hand, determined to continue her role as a virgin.

Sir reached into his jacket and pulled out a velvet box. "A test." He opened it and held up a long strand of pearls. He placed the strand over either side of her clit and pulled the necklace taut so that the pearls caressed both sides of her sensitive nub, then he slowly pulled the strand down. Each individual pearl rubbed against her clit as it passed. She appreciated the length of the necklace as she squirmed under its sensual caress. When he reached the end, he repositioned it and dragged it down again. Brie moaned softly in pleasure, trying not to behave as wantonly as she felt.

He held up the strand of pearls and twisted them once, then placed them over her head and laid them on her chest. She felt the moistness of her excitement on the jewelry.

Sir slipped his hand in between her eager pussy lips, his fingers sliding over her clit leisurely. She tried to remain still in order to pass the 'test', although she coveted his touch.

"Girl, it's time to expose the truth." She whimpered when he slowly inserted his middle finger inside her. He swirled it over the smooth walls of her vagina and her body inadvertently moved with him, ravenous for his attention. "For an innocent, you are exceedingly wet."

"You have that effect on me, Sir," she whispered.

With his finger stroking her from the inside, he corrected, "Khan."

Brie blushed, realizing she'd slipped out of character. She licked her lips, ready to apologize, when he hit her G-spot. She groaned, her body automatically arching in pleasure. A fire instantly ignited, one she did not have control over. She shook her head, trying to keep the orgasm at bay. It was too soon, since she was playing a virgin. "No, no…"

"Do not deny me."

She opened her eyes and looked into Sir's as the chill took over and her nipples hardened. A small cry escaped her lips as her muscles caressed his finger in their undulating rhythm. He growled under his breath, his eyes gleaming with lust.

He pulled his finger out and tasted her. "Sweet as an innocent should be."

Brie lay there staring at him, totally enamored by the man. Again, she thought Sir might take her then, but he instructed her to dress. She sat up and slowly zipped her gown. "Pearls underneath," Sir instructed.

She glanced at the boy, who had witnessed the whole scene. He stared at her intently, but remained where he was.

Sir tied her wrists behind her back again and covered her shoulders with the fur. The limousine pulled up to an opulent theater famous for its operatic performances. Sir helped Brie out of the vehicle and told the young man to follow.

It thrilled Brie to be bound in public and not have anyone aware of it. People nodded at the attractive couple, with no idea of the plans Sir had for Brie. She held her head up proudly, honored to be seen with Sir, excited to be his submissive for the evening.

He took her to a private box and ushered the boy in. He directed Brie to the seat nearest the stage. Sir sat next to her and the young man stood in the shadows. Brie wondered when Sir would reveal the boy's purpose.

Sir leaned over and slid the fur off her shoulders before untying her wrists. "Have you been to an opera before?"

"Khan, may I be brutally honest?"

"Yes," he answered with a smirk.

"I have avoided them. I'm not into foreign singing."

"You have done yourself a grave disservice, girl. Have you heard the story of Madame Butterfly?"

"I only know it ends sadly."

"Indeed. Unrequited love that ends in tragedy."

As if on cue, the lights went down and the opera began. Brie enjoyed the costumes and the elaborate set, but it was the soulful voice of the girl that moved her. The tender and consuming love the girl expressed for her indifferent husband touched Brie's heart, and she felt tears prick her eyes.

"Girl!"

She turned to Sir, realizing she hadn't heard him calling her name. "Yes, Khan?"

"Over my knee, now."

Brie lay down over his muscular thighs and felt Sir pull her dress up over her waist. The darkness gave them the illusion of privacy, although anyone in the adjacent boxes would be able to see what he was doing if he or she simply stood up.

His warm hand caressed her ass, soothingly, teasingly… She closed her eyes, enjoying his sensual touch. When he lifted his hand, she held her breath. It came down forcefully but without pain. Instead, the contact reverberated through her loins. His swats were slow, solid and controlled, meant solely to arouse—his was a powerful, masculine caress that possessed her body and soul.

He fisted her hair and pulled her head back, kissing her with more than just passion. Brie responded, communicating her love for him through her lips. He pulled away abruptly and commanded, "Stand."

Sir moved the chairs to the side and ordered her to lie on her back. She eagerly complied, thrilled when he lay beside her. He unzipped her dress, playing with the pearls hidden underneath. There in the dark, with the music echoing through the theater, Sir readied himself to take his devoted sub. Only, he didn't…

Once he had unclasped her bra, Sir motioned the boy over—her priest. She was naked except for her garter belt, hose and heels, her legs wide open to him. The angel-faced boy knelt before her, undoing his buckle before unzipping his pants. He freed his long, hard member and began stroking it. Brie's loins tingled. She knew he was about to take her, but she wanted it to be Sir. *Screw my fantasy!*

Sir began caressing her body as he licked and nibbled her breasts. She responded to his attention, but stiffened when she felt the boy's hand on her. Sir looked up and commanded, "Let him touch you."

Brie forced herself to relax as the young man explored her soft folds with his fingers, lightly flicking her clit. She jumped when she felt the warmth of his tongue.

"Prove yourself worthy of your Khan's attention," Sir ordered.

His words changed her perception. This was her fantasy that Sir had thoughtfully set up. Instead of fighting off the boy's attention, she allowed herself to yearn for it. Brie opened to the boy and felt the fire begin to build. The whole time, Sir ravished her with his hands and mouth. It was the best of all worlds. Two men focused on her pleasure, demanding her orgasm.

The music was building up to a crescendo, just like her body. Sir leaned over and whispered in her ear, "Let him take your innocence." His lips came down on hers, his tongue entering her mouth at the same moment the blond penetrated her with his lengthy cock.

Brie forgot she was in public and cried out. Then she kissed Sir fiercely, releasing all the love and passion she had built up over the weeks. He groaned into her mouth, returning the intensity as the boy rammed his cock deep and hard—the three of them a ball of human lust. Sir bit her neck, sending ribbons of electricity to her groin.

She threw her head back and moaned. The music matched the fervor churning inside her, and then the chills began. Sir leaned over her possessively. Even in the dark, she swore she could see love expressed in his gaze.

"I want you to come for him." He locked lips with her as Brie's body stiffened and then shuddered in a forceful release—all the passion, all the love mixing into the physical embodiment of pleasure. It was a feeling like no other, and she embraced the climax to the very last spasm.

Sir pulled away from her and his expression changed as he reconstructed the wall between them. She could sense the distance he was creating, but was powerless to stop it.

The boy distracted her by kissing her thighs tenderly in gratitude. She appreciated the sweet gesture, but could only stare at the intricately carved ceiling, wondering if her heart could take any more games.

Sir helped Brie dress before the intermission. She'd barely had her dress zipped before soft lights illuminated their box. She was shaken by the intensity of their encounter and sat in her chair, pretending to watch the crowd of people milling below.

Sir turned to the boy and whispered something. Brie glanced over and saw the young man nod to him and then give her a meaningful glance before exiting the balcony. Sir turned to her and held out his hand. "We are done here, unless you want to watch Butterfly commit *jisatsu.*"

Brie popped out of her seat and took his hand hastily. He pulled her to him, bringing their lips within centimeters of each other, but then he slowly turned her to face away from him. His hands ran down her arms and then grasped her wrists forcefully. He bound them and covered her with the fur, biting her neck lightly in the process. They left the theater just as the last act began.

The limousine was waiting for them outside. She noticed the blond was nowhere to be seen. It was just Brie and Sir... Her heart began to race as she thought of the possibilities.

Sir buckled her in and sat opposite her, just as he had at the beginning of the evening. She watched him covertly, hoping he would finally make his move.

"What did you think of the opera, girl?"

Still playing his role...

"It was more beautiful than I expected and," she paused and looked him directly in the eye, "far more exciting, Khan."

He had a slight smirk on his face. "Now that we have your deflowering out of the way, I can use you however I see fit."

She felt delightful shivers run down her spine. "Yes, most revered Khan. I am yours for the taking."

"After I untie you, remove your dress and bra. Brace your waist against the seat. I don't plan to be gentle."

Brie's whole body trembled with excitement. She followed his instructions and laid her stomach against the seat with her legs spread wide for him. She whimpered softly when she felt his hand grasp her sex.

"Mine!"

He trailed his hands over her body, seeming to relish every inch. Then he grabbed her ass with one hand and guided his cock with the other, rubbing and teasing her moist lips. He tormented her with his manhood, arousing her desire to greater heights. She wiggled against his rigid shaft, *needing* him to take her with that princely cock.

"You want this, girl?" She felt Sir move into position, his shaft ready to penetrate her soul.

"Yes! Love me hard, Khan," she cried.

He pushed violently away from her.

"I do not love," he growled. Sir moved back to his seat and sat there in silence.

She braved a peek and saw him staring intensely at her. "I'm sorry, Sir. It was a bad choice of words."

His whole countenance changed and the trainer returned. "Miss Bennett…" Oh, how Brie hated it when he called her by her last name. "You cannot confuse the emotions of a scene for real life."

"Sir, I…"

"Enough. We are done for the evening."

They spent the rest of the car ride in silence. Brie was sure she'd seen love smoldering behind his gaze at the theater, and she had certainly felt it in his kisses. She hadn't been imagining things and there was no way it had been part of the 'scene'. Why couldn't Sir forget the rules for one night and love her body, the way they both wanted—both needed?

When the limo pulled up to her apartment Sir said, "Although the fur comes with me, the rest is yours to keep. Have a good evening, Miss Bennett."

"Thank you, Sir."

Brie got out of the limo, feeling shell-shocked. How could the evening be ending like this? Everything had been so promising, so deliciously exciting. She could still feel Sir's passionate lips pressed against hers.

As she watched the limousine exit the parking lot, she lifted the pearls out from under her dress and dragged them across her teeth. *Whatever it takes, I will get you to say those three words tomorrow, Sir. I've been patient long enough.*

Preparing for Graduation

B rie walked into Sir's office, a tangle of nerves. The night before graduation, each girl was expected to sit down with Sir to discuss their overall experience with the program, as well as their plans for the future. It was her best chance, and perhaps her only chance to get him to admit his true feelings. Really, now that their graduation was imminent, there was no reason for him to hide it any longer.

"Please sit," Sir said in his smooth, velvety voice.

Brie sat down and thrust her hands between her legs to keep them still, not wanting to expose her tense excitement. She looked him directly in the eyes, letting her face express her love for him.

He cleared his throat. *A sign of his own nervous excitement?* she wondered gleefully. "I am assuming you still seek to be collared tomorrow?"

She beamed. "Yes, Sir."

"I thought so. It's a wise choice for you. Although you have the ability to please the Dom you are with, I don't think you will truly be satisfied until you can focus on a single Master."

Brie couldn't stop herself from smiling. "I long for it, Sir."

"I shall be forthright with you, Miss Bennett. You are one of the most talented subs I have had the pleasure to instruct. Although your instincts get in the way at times, you have the ability to please and charm a variety of Dominants. It has been satisfying to witness. However, I have enjoyed your wit, coupled with your fearless determination, that much more."

"Thank you, Sir," she purred, bursting with happiness. "I've flourished under your instruction."

He waved the compliment away, choosing instead to splash cold water on their exchange. "You have two noteworthy Doms who are interested in you. I have confidence both would care for you well, although they couldn't be further from each other in philosophy."

Brie shook her head. What was he talking about? *Two?*

He read the confusion on her face and responded, "Am I wrong to assume you will be choosing between Nosaka and Wallace?"

A nervous giggle escaped from her lips. "Those are not the only two."

His tone became deadly serious. "Miss Bennett... I hope you are not under the impression that trainers are an option. I told you early on that we cannot partner with our students."

She stammered, "But... I... We graduate tomorrow."

His expression changed into one of compassion. "I

will always be your trainer. Your graduation does not change that. Feel free to come to me or any of the trainers if you ever have need. We will always be here for you."

She stared at him dully, trying to process his words. In one fell swoop, he'd stripped away two of her choices. No Marquis and no...Sir. The ice-cold reality of what he was saying washed over her.

A pained look traveled across his face before he spoke. "Miss Bennett, I thought you understood."

She shook her head slowly.

Within a few seconds the worried look on his face transformed into a reassuring smile. "Well, there is no reason to be upset." He picked up a pen from his desk and began fiddling with it. "You have two exceptional Doms to choose from. Ren Nosaka is a master at his skill. It is obvious that he has feelings for you. As for Todd Wallace, I had my reservations when he approached the Center about wanting to train as a Dom. However, he has proven himself to me. In fact..." Sir looked at her intently. "I see some of myself in him. That's why I chose to spend time outside the Center instructing Mr. Wallace. Although I am not a master of one particular area, I have a solid background overall. It's the main reason I was chosen as headmaster of the Center."

Brie couldn't believe that the man who had trained do everything was the one man who chose to rely solely on his touch. It made him...perfect.

"I am unsure if Mr. Wallace is simply infatuated with you, but that is something the two of you can explore if you choose." Sir's eyes were gentle, so loving.

A tear escaped and slowly trailed down her cheek.

It seemed as if he couldn't handle seeing it, so he chose to ignore it by saying, "You are in a win-win situation, Miss Bennett." Sir pulled a photo out of his desk and placed it in front of her. It was the one that Tono had taken of her. "Any man who can make you feel this way is worthy."

She stared at him, still in shock. He continued on, choosing to be oblivious of her pain. "Mr. Wallace, on the other hand, can provide you with a variety of experiences. He seems to have an innate talent, one that cannot be taught. I feel he has the capability to stretch you, and that is an important consideration."

He put the pen down and gazed at her. "The choice is up to you. You can partner with a man you obviously have a connection with or a Dom who has the same desire to grow. Trust that instinct of yours, Miss Bennett. You cannot make a wrong choice if you do."

How could he deny his feelings for her? Brie wondered if there was something she could do at the ceremony, but he interrupted her thoughts. "If someone were foolish enough to present me with a collar, I would be forced to reject it."

She stared at him in misery.

"It is important to concentrate on the viable options afforded you, Miss Bennett. Don't allow anything to distract you from that decision."

"But Sir, I..."

He held up his hand to silence her declaration of love and then pointed to the collar around her neck. "It is no longer needed. Come." He gestured to the floor at his feet.

Her body was leaden as she got up from the chair and bowed before him. She closed her eyes as he unfastened the collar. She felt a chill as the warmth of the leather was replaced by the coolness of the air and a sob escaped her lips.

He placed it on his desk and said quietly, "You may leave. You have much to consider tonight. I will explain to the others that you were unexpectedly called away."

She stood up unsteadily.

"Miss Bennett, this is for the best."

Somehow, Brie made it out of his office, but she stumbled in her six-inch heels. She angrily ripped them off her feet, throwing them across the hall with a growl. Then the tears came. She pressed her face against the wall, sobbing uncontrollably.

She heard him clear his throat several times and held her breath, staring at the open door, hoping he would come for her. When that did not happen, she slowly picked up her shoes and walked to the classroom to retrieve her coat and purse. In a trance, she left the Center and headed home.

When Brie made it to her apartment, she walked inside without turning the lights on. She collapsed on the bed with her hands covering her ears in a feeble attempt to shut out the world.

She woke up the next morning to bright sunlight and a feeling of hope. Then she remembered the night before and her joy faltered. She focused on the wax mold Tono had created of her. Despite the fact Sir could never be hers, Brie did have two men she cared for.

There was no doubt she loved Tono. Just thinking about him gave her pleasant shivers. A relationship with Tono would be full of amazing sex, delicious bondage, and maybe even a side career in Kinbaku. He respected and loved her, and she him. Truly, in every way he was a perfect choice.

Then there was Faelan. She laughed when she thought of Blue Eyes. He was young like she was, as well as determined and innately talented. He had an adventurous spirit and the wildness to challenge Brie beyond her comfort level. That excited her. His dangerous component and the animal chemistry they shared made him a viable option. They could learn and grow as one, doing God only knew what to each other. A match made in heaven.

Brie sighed. Unfortunately, both Doms also had their drawbacks.

Tono was a Kinbaku master. That meant his expertise was limited. Not only that, but he had a kind soul. She couldn't see him picking up a cane and giving her convincing whacks with it. What if there came a time she needed that?

Faelan, on the other hand, was young, and as inexperienced as she was. Brie hadn't decided yet if she loved him. It could be a case of animal magnetism and nothing more. Plus, she didn't like the fact all the submissives at the Center wanted the new Dom. Brie desired an exclusive relationship—no harems allowed.

At least she still had the interviews. She felt certain comparing the two side by side would help her make a definitive decision.

Brie spent the day preparing her body for the graduation ceremony. She went to a salon and got her hair and nails done professionally. She handed the hairdresser a beautiful comb she had picked out especially for the evening. It was a silver and gold abstract representation of a wolf; a symbol of Faelan.

When she got back to her apartment she began to dress in an outfit she'd assembled specifically to attract her Master. Brie held up the scarlet corset covered in black lace. It had cost her more than a hundred dollars, but was definitely worth it. Once she'd put it on, the enchanting corset showed off her shapely figure, but didn't cut into her skin when the laces were pulled tight. She slipped on her expensive hose and attached them to her lacy garter belt. The hose were a sheer black material that shimmered in the light. Her skirt came next. It was a black lace micro number that swished against her butt cheeks when she walked. She had also chosen a golden chain that hung around her hips seductively.

Brie twirled in front of the mirror. Nothing said sex and class like the color black, but it was the scarlet of her corset that made her deliciously alluring. *Oh, yeah! Come to me, Master…*

A few minutes before she left, Brie put on her shoes. She'd gone with the traditional six-inch height, but these shoes were stunning. They were all black except for the heels, which were ornately decorated with metallic gold. Totally hot!

There was only one more piece needed to complete her look. Brie carefully slipped the bracelet onto her forearm. The gold dragon wound around her arm seductively and gave her a slave girl image she liked. Naturally, the dragon was her symbol for Tono.

Neither Dom would suspect she held a piece of each of them for luck. She glanced in the mirror one more time... *Perfect.*

The Interviews Begin

The school parking lot was jam-packed when she pulled up. Apparently, tons of people from the D/s community had come to celebrate the latest graduates. Brie suddenly felt shy and snuck around the back.

She walked through the empty hallways until she saw Lea. Then she made a beeline towards her, hugging Lea from behind. "Can you believe it, girl? *We* are graduates!"

"I know!" Lea grinned, turning around to look at her. "To think of all that we've been through to get to this point. And did you see how many Dominants came to check us out?"

"Oh... Is that why so many people are here tonight?"

"Ms. Clark said that half the people are old alumni and the other half are Doms looking for a partner."

"I guess you're going to have fun tonight!"

Lea turned her around several times, looking her up and down. "Wow, Brie. You look incredible."

"So do you, Lea," she said, complimenting Lea's purple, fairy-like outfit with a wide scoop neck that showed off her ample bosom.

"No, seriously, Brie… You look stunning."

She shrugged. "How else should I look for my Master?"

"Have you decided then?" Lea asked in a low whisper.

Brie shook her head. "Not yet, although I am definitely leaning in one direction."

"I bet I know who it is!" Lea answered, giving Brie a tight squeeze.

Brie was about to ask Lea which one she thought when Mary came up, looking drop-dead gorgeous in a latex catsuit. The woman had the right body to fill out every naughty curve. "Still planning to ruin your fun, huh?"

"If you are asking if I still plan to get collared tonight, the answer is yes."

Mary's smile turned into an ugly frown. "Well, I always knew you were an idiot. Now the whole D/s community will know it as well. Me? I plan to shop around. I've heard there are a few foreigners lurking about tonight. I plan to get me a little of that action." She slapped Brie's face playfully. "So should you."

Three of the trainers came to the back area to talk to the graduates. Each had been assigned a specific girl to watch over for the evening. Luckily for Brie, Marquis Gray was her escort. She was surprised to see a submissive standing beside him. She was an older woman with long, black hair and pale blue eyes. Marquis introduced her to Brie. "Miss Bennett, this is my submissive, Celestia."

So, Marquis Gray was never an option. How conceited am I?

Brie took the woman's hand in hers. "It is a pleasure to meet you, Celestia." She wanted to add, "You lucky sub, you!" but just smiled and squeezed Celestia's hand lightly.

Marquis informed Brie, "Tonight you will be spending time with the D/s community at large. Feel free to speak with whomever you want. People are here to celebrate your accomplishment as well as to meet you in person. You have thirty minutes before I ask who you want to meet with first."

"Thank you, Marquis Gray."

"Headmaster Davis will announce each of the graduates in turn, starting with you. Stand beside him and then move to the left when he calls the next name. Once all three of you have been introduced, you will be free to socialize."

Brie waited for her name and entered the large commons on cue. She was stunned at the number of people crowding the elaborately decorated room. The commons looked grand and elegant. Leave it to the Submissive Training Center to send their subs out in style.

She stood next to Sir. It wasn't as hard being near him as it had been in the past. Knowing he could never be hers had tempered her feelings somehow. She smiled serenely as he announced her name to the community and added, "As many of you know, this class of submissives graduated with the highest overall scores in our school's distinguished history. Miss Bennett was head of her class." There was a polite round of applause.

When it died down, Sir took her hand and shook it twice, saying, "Well done, Miss Bennett." His expression was one of pride but no intimacy. He let go and then announced Lea's name.

Brie moved to the left, where Mr. Gallant handed her a plaque and shook her hand warmly. "Well done, Miss Bennett. We are all proud of your unrivaled success."

She bowed and whispered, "I couldn't have done it without you, Teacher."

He blessed her with a proud smile and then readied himself to hand Lea her plaque. Brie stood there, discreetly looking over the crowd. She saw Tono standing alone, looking devastatingly handsome in his dark suit. His midnight hair covered his left eye in a devilishly flirtatious fashion. Any reservations she'd felt about him disappeared when he smiled.

After the short ceremony had ended, the two of them walked towards each other as if drawn together by a magnet. His hand caressed her cheek as he leaned in and murmured, "You are stunning, toriko."

She pressed her face into his hand, looking deep into his brown eyes. "You take my breath away, Tono."

"Exactly the response I was looking for, little slave. Will you dance with me?"

It was strange to have this new dynamic between them. They were not playing a scene and this was not a training session.

She took his hand and he led her out to the middle of the floor, placing one hand behind her back while grasping her right hand with the other. He guided her around the dance floor in a fluid motion. Brie was pleasantly surprised she could stay in step with him simply by looking into his magnetic eyes.

"I have a surprise for you."

She grinned. "Oh, what? I love surprises!"

He nodded to a small man standing off to the side. A man who was watching them with scary intensity. "My father has come from the homeland to meet you."

Brie hadn't made her final decision yet and stammered, "Tono, I am not a hundred percent sure I can make a decision tonight."

He chuckled lightly. "It's okay. My father insisted on being present at your graduation. I have spoken so much about you that he wanted to see your rare beauty for himself."

She sighed as she looked at the unsmiling man.

Tono lifted her chin to bring her back into connection with him, before twirling her around and lightly catching her in his arms. She let the crowd fall away as Tono swept her into his rhythm. "I will be asked to meet with you tonight," he stated, rather than asked.

Brie pressed her cheek against his chest. "Of course, Tono."

"May I ask who else?"

She hesitated to answer, but looked up and smiled. "I only plan to ask one other."

"The boy?"

She stifled a giggle. Funny to think that the other Doms had nicknamed Todd 'the Boy'. It wasn't the first time she'd heard it. Brie had a suspicion Todd Wallace would quickly change their tune. "Yes, Tono, the other meeting will be with Faelan."

He did not mince words. "Do you love the boy?"

She looked down at their feet and became distracted by the graceful way they moved together. "I do feel something for him," she muttered softly.

He continued dancing but said nothing. When the music stopped, he guided her over to his father. Brie tried to keep her composure, relying on her basic sub training—eyes to the ground and the body in a pleasing but respectful position.

Tono bowed low before his father and said, his voice ripe with respect, "*Otosama*, this is Miss Brianna Bennett."

She bowed and waited, with her eyes glued to her toes. Only silence followed, but she could feel the old man's gaze on her as he studied her carefully. His callused fingers grasped her chin and he lifted her eyes to meet his. He had the same chocolate brown eyes, but they were cold; not like Tono's at all. She struggled not to shiver against his hand.

The old man pushed his nose to within an inch from her face and stared into her eyes as if he was searching for something specific, something he could only see upon closer inspection. She allowed his invasion, hoping he would find what he needed to approve of her.

After several uncomfortable moments he let go of her chin and turned to Tono. He said only one word in Japanese: "*Dame.*" Then he walked away.

Tono shook his head as if to clear it. He looked at Brie and offered her a reassuring smile before heading off after his father.

She wanted to yell, "What does it mean, Tono?"

However, she remembered her place and allowed him to leave without knowing why.

Brie watched Mary cozying up to a flamboyant Spaniard. He seemed quite taken with her. Although he did have the prettiest gray eyes Brie had ever seen, he wasn't nearly manly enough to be attractive to Brie. Mary could have him.

Lea had found their mutual 'doctor' friend, Master Harris. The two seemed to be hitting it off well, and Brie wondered again if something might happen between them. Both had great senses of humor and it made her smile to think of them together.

Faelan came up from behind and growled in her ear. "I may have missed out on the first dance, but I insist on the next."

She turned around and smiled coyly. "I was saving the best for last." He looked youthfully debonair in dark clothes with a gray shirt, of which he had rolled up the sleeves just enough to expose his strong, veiny arms.

"Don't you forget that, blossom. I may lack Tono's elderly status, but I can take you places he never will." As proof, Faelan moved the hair away from her neck and kissed that tantalizing spot where her shoulder and neck met. He easily lulled her into his seduction. Brie's body responded without shame, remembering their chocolate 'dance'. There was no doubt her body liked Faelan *very* much.

"Who else is my competition?" he asked, moving to the other side of her neck, holding her tightly when her knees threatened to give out.

"Just Tono…" Brie breathed out.

"Good, then your choice is between the wise old owl and the eager young wolf. Seems simple enough to me."

She slapped him on the ass. "I think you mean the arrogant wolf pup."

Faelan grabbed the back of her head with one hand and her chin with the other. He kissed her, then, like she had never been kissed before. The possessiveness behind his embrace instantly made her wet and desperate for him.

He left Brie gasping for air when he let go. "Confidence, blossom, not arrogance."

She excused herself, needing some distance between them to reorient herself. She looked across the room and saw Mr. Gallant with a sleek, dark woman of Amazon stature. The possessive hold he had around her waist left no doubt the Amazon was his wife. The height difference between the two was adorable, yet even so, Mr. Gallant looked every part the Dom and she the willing and happy submissive.

Ms. Clark headed towards Brie, so she braced herself for a confrontation. There was no need. The trainer passed by on her way to talk to Lea. After a brief conversation, Ms. Clark approached Master Harris. The interviews were beginning.

She jumped when Marquis appeared at her side, as if out of nowhere. "Are you ready for your first meeting?"

Brie was unable to hide the fear crowding her heart. "Marquis Gray, Tono was supposed to be my first, but he went to chase after his father." She pointed in the direction the two had disappeared. "Do you have any idea what '*dame*' means in Japanese?"

His lips formed a thin line. "Not good."

"What do you mean by that? Did I do something wrong?"

He looked down at her without any expression in his dark eyes. "No, Miss Bennett. That is simply what the word means."

Brie felt herself falling backwards. *Not good?*

Marquis took her by the arm and guided her towards the room they had assigned for Brie's interviews. "Forget it for now. Concentrate on the next Dom you want to meet with."

She looked back in the direction in which Tono had left. "But I don't understand…"

"Miss Bennett, listen to me. You cannot waste this opportunity. Who would you like me to bring to your first meeting?"

"Faelan," she answered distractedly.

"Fine. I will find Mr. Wallace. Go inside and wait, but I caution you to concentrate on what you are going to ask Mr. Wallace when he gets here. Do not waste energy wondering about what happened earlier."

She nodded her head numbly, feeling crushed by the encounter with Tono's father. Marquis Gray grabbed her shoulders. "Do you understand me, pearl?"

His forceful nature brought her back, and she answered with a quiet, "Yes." Before she walked into the room she added, "Thank you, Master Gray."

He gave her an uncharacteristic wink and left. Brie felt sad knowing that she would not spend time with Marquis after this. Everything was ending—*everything…* She sat down on the leather couch, trying not to let the weight of it consume her.

Brie listened instead to the exuberant laughter and music just outside the door, and reminded herself that this was a celebration. A celebration of her success.

Faelan walked in with a smile that was both provocative and charming. "Good evening, Graduate."

She actually blushed and sputtered, "When do you guys graduate?"

"Our ceremony is a…more private affair."

"Oh, really?"

"Sorry, no details. Only Dominants are worthy of the specifics."

Brie opened her mouth in protest and then closed it with a wicked grin. "Maybe I need to go to Dominant school next."

He swept down on her and crushed Brie against the couch. "Oh, no. You are perfect just as you are."

She laughed, struggling to breathe. He deftly rolled her on top of him and watched her reaction as his cock ballooned between them. Faelan was definitely male in every sense of the word.

Brie pretended not to notice and started the official interview, ignoring his lustful stare. "So, Mr. Wallace, I must first ask how old you are."

"Twenty-five."

"Ah, I see." Brie smiled at knowing he was only three years older. "What exactly do you do for a living, besides dominating innocent subs, that is?"

"I'm an assistant manager of a department store. It may not be glamorous work, but it pays the bills and I plan to advance myself onto bigger and better things."

"Managerial position, huh? I suppose that's a fitting career choice for a Dom." She tapped his nose and asked, "How would you feel about a submissive who has a career of her own? Say a film career?"

"It isn't a problem unless your career includes lots of travel and months away from me. If that's the case, I could not give my approval. The whole reason I want you is so we can spend time together, blossom."

His words concerned Brie. Filming was not a nine-to-five desk job. She could go anywhere in the world at any time. It was all dependent on the project. "We may have a problem then, Faelan." Brie got off his lap and stood up. This was serious business. This was her future they were talking about.

He wouldn't let her go so easily and wrapped his powerful arms around her, pulling her back onto him. He growled in her ear, "I am sure we can work something out. Even if it means me coming to dominate my girl on weekends."

She squirmed in pleasure when he nibbled on her earlobe, but resisted further teasing. Brie pushed herself up on his chest and told him, in no uncertain terms, "This is important. If you can't support my need to become a film director, I really don't see this working between us."

He snorted in anger. "Did you not just hear me? I said we would find a way to make it work." Then he growled in a low, deep tone, "But only if you wear a tight corset under your clothes and promise to come every day at designated times while you are away from me."

She liked the suggestion and rubbed his scruffy chin.

"Are you sure you would be willing to support me in this? I might not make it for a while, and you'll have to put up with a starving artist in the meantime. It kind of goes with the territory of artsy-fartsy types like me."

He kissed her roughly, but when he pulled away she blurted, "What if I become wildly successful?" She grimaced as she wondered aloud, "Can a Dominant handle his sub making more money than he is…?"

"Enough, blossom. I accept you for who you are. We will work out the logistics like any couple must. I want you." His hands ran down her sides. "I want to dominate this body in every way known to man, and then add a few of my own." He bit her neck and she melted into him.

"Not fair…" she whimpered, her loins contracting in pleasure as he changed positions and pushed her down on the couch.

"If I could, I would collar you right now." He fumbled with his pants before he ripped her panties aside. She gasped as the round head of his cock penetrated her with persuasive force. He felt so good inside her.

Faelan thrust deeply, leaving no doubt that he was claiming his territory. "I feel you awakening, blossom," he murmured.

It was true—her body was giving itself over to the wildness he provoked. "I can't. Not here, not yet," she complained, trying to push off the couch.

"You can and you will."

"But I'm not done interviewing you. Are you thinking twenty-four-hour submission or just several times a week?"

"You with me, twenty-four seven," he answered, nibbling her collarbone as he pumped deep into her.

"Living where?" she gasped as he bit down harder.

"My place, of course. I've set it up for us, my sweet."

She almost let herself go, but reined the reaction in just in time to complain, "But you live fifty minutes from my work."

"Stay at the tobacco shop or find a job closer. It matters little to me…" He began sucking on her skin, causing a delightful, concentrated burn.

"Stop, Faelan," she protested weakly, as her body betrayed her and gave in to his desire.

"You want me, blossom. You *need* me," he snarled into her neck, licking and biting her.

Control was almost his, but she forced out one more question. "Do you see this as temporary or long-term?"

He stopped thrusting and looked at her. "Is there any question?" He went to bite her ear, but she stopped him.

"Answering a question with a question is *not* an answer."

He smiled a wolfish grin. "I want to devour you for a lifetime."

"But if it doesn't work between us?" she cautioned.

"I will howl to the moon in frustration." He belted a long howl before pulling out and descending between her legs. Brie giggled, cried out and then screamed for mercy as he devoured his prize.

She looked up at the ceiling as her body fought against wave after wave of pleasure. Finally, she had no more fight left and relaxed. Brie let out a low-pitched growl as her pent-up frustration released in a lightning bolt of orgasmic force.

"Good, blossom. I like to see your animal," Faelan complimented as he patted her mound and then lay on top of her, crushing her with his weight. "You cannot resist the power of your potential mate, the commander of your soul."

Breathless from the weight of his body on her chest, she gasped out, "I have not... decided...anything...Faelan."

"But you *will*. Tonight is the night. I feel it in my bones." He lifted himself off her and sat down on the couch, gathering her onto his lap. "It is easy to see your desire to be collared tonight. The question is, which man will be found deserving of such a prize?" He tweaked her nose. "In case you were wondering, I *am* that man."

The bell sounded, the one that let the girls know that there were only ten minutes left of the first session. Brie looked at Faelan and smiled. "How may I please you, Lord?"

"Lord Faelan..." He said the name again, letting it roll on his tongue. "I could get used to that, woman."

Brie knelt before him. "Your pleasure, Lord Faelan?"

He stood up, his cock a sword before her. "I would like to fuck your red lips, blossom."

"My red lips shall love you well, my Lord." She grasped his shaft and opened her mouth wide to wrap him in her warmth.

He groaned appreciatively and placed his hand on her head, helping to guide her. It was her turn to moan as she gave in to the joy of being his. She pushed the head of his shaft to the back of her throat and relaxed her muscles. She took one more quick breath before sliding it farther in.

"Oh, my blossom…" he grunted huskily.

She moaned around his cock as she pushed her lips to the base of his manhood. With a gentle rocking motion, she caressed his shaft with her tight throat muscles and then drew him out to lick and suck the head again.

"Oh, fuck, woman."

She looked up at him and purred. She took him fully again, this time rocking with more motion, causing her throat to tighten. She actually thought she heard the man squeak.

He must have heard himself, because he suddenly grabbed her hair and started pumping his cock into her, grunting in a deep, masculine way. She would have found it amusing, but then he spoke. "Those red lips on my cock. The tightness of your throat, the depth. Such perfection…"

She felt soulful satisfaction when his body stiffened and his essence shot deep into her throat. *The heaven I can share with him.*

He stroked her soft curls and murmured, "My beautiful, talented blossom."

She glanced up at Faelan and was touched by the tender look in his eye. This was the man who had rescued her from the pavement and then spent his nights becoming the best Dominant possible in order to be compatible with her. Sir had believed in him enough to take extra time to train the boy—as if Faelan was his gift to her.

She broke the suction on Faelan's cock and kissed the tip before standing up. She could see herself becoming his. He was young, energetic, inquisitive, sexy, with that hint of danger she found addictive.

As Brie straightened herself for the next meeting, she prayed desperately that Tono would be waiting for her. She needed to talk to him, to see where they stood, before she could make a decision.

The final bell sounded. Brie took Faelan's hand and walked him out of the room. She noticed Mary come out at the same time with the tall Spaniard. The Spaniard Dom kissed her hand gallantly and left.

Faelan nibbled Brie's ear as his final goodbye and whispered, "I'll be waiting, blossom."

Brie watched him leave and then scanned the crowd for Tono. She let out a nervous sigh when she didn't see him and shifted her gaze to Mary.

Master Coen came up to Mary and she whispered a name. He nodded and went to fetch the next Dom. Mary looked in Brie's direction and gave her a funny smile, shrugging her shoulders.

"How's it going?" Brie asked.

Mary didn't answer. She just disappeared into the room to wait for her Dom.

It Gets Complicated

Brie didn't know who else to interview. She glanced over the gathering, looking for a face that stood out from the crowd of foreign Dominants. Her jaw dropped when she saw Faelan walking with Master Coen to Mary's room. *What the hell, Mary?*

Faelan looked at her apologetically as he passed by. She understood. He was not allowed to turn down Mary's request. It was part of the rules for the evening. The submissives were allowed to ask whomever they wanted without fear of rejection. *Fuck the damn rules!* Brie wanted to grab Blue Eyes by the hand and pull him away from the temptress-turned-backstabber.

Instead, she stood mutely by as Faelan entered Mary's room and shut the door behind him. Could the evening get any worse?

Marquis Gray was by her side, asking for her next Dom. She muttered sadly, "I have no one else."

"Surely there is someone who has caught your eye, Miss Bennett. Do not waste even one meeting tonight."

Brie glanced over at Sir. He looked good in the expensive Italian tux he wore for the occasion. His face was relaxed and his smile radiant as he laughed at some joke a group of admiring submissives had made. Brie thought it cute the way his hands danced in the air as he talked.

She looked away and answered, "No. There is no one else…" She glanced at the door Mary and Faelan were behind and forced herself not to scream.

"You must pick someone," Marquis Gray insisted.

"Fine." She looked up at him. "Then I choose you."

He seemed shocked. "You can't choose me. Trainers are not allowed."

Brie pouted. "But I'm not asking you to collar me, Marquis Gray."

"What would be the point?" he protested.

"I need you," she said quietly, turning away to hide her misery.

He was silent for a moment and then excused himself. She secretly observed him as he walked over to his submissive and the two had a short discussion. The woman followed him back to Brie. "Celestia has agreed to join us, if you have no objections."

Brie glanced at the older woman and smiled. "I have no objections, Marquis Gray."

"Fine." Marquis guided both of them into the room. He left the door open, which Brie found odd but did not question.

He gestured her to the couch while his submissive settled down at his feet. Brie couldn't help feeling jealous of her.

"What would you like to discuss?"

Brie's eyes opened wide when she heard Mary's passionate scream ring out from the other room, and she shut her mouth, refusing to speak.

"I know what you need, pearl." Marquis Gray whispered something to his partner, and she gracefully stood up and left the room. "Take off your corset and shoes. Leave everything else on."

With shaking hands she removed the few items he required, trying not to think about what was going on with Mary.

Marquis Gray commanded her full attention. "On your knees, facing away from the door. I want you to look at me."

She knelt down on the mat in the middle of the room and watched as he took off his jacket and shirt, then tossed them on the couch. She stared up at him, but flinched when she heard Mary cry out again.

"Ask me a question," Marquis Gray insisted.

Brie forced her brain to think, sifting through the fog of her jealousy. Her first question to Faelan popped into her head and she asked, "How old are you?"

Marquis smirked. "Thirty-nine. How much older does that make me?"

She had to concentrate hard to do the simple math. "That makes you seventeen years older."

"Very good, pearl. Nice to know your public education has amounted to something." It took a few seconds for her to register he'd made a joke.

Celestia returned with a flogger and lace. Brie took in a deep breath, grateful he had read her undisclosed desire.

Marquis Gray took the items and knelt beside Brie. He tied the black lace over her eyes, murmuring softly, "Remember our first night, pearl? You were kneeling on that stage, a bundle of nerves but determined to show the world what a superior sub you were." He chuckled warmly. "You have succeeded in impressing all of the panel, young lady, even those set against you."

He stood up and she heard something drag across the floor. "Lean your torso against the ottoman."

She did as he asked, anxious for the thud of the flogger against her skin to drown out the occasional noises coming from the other room. He swept her hair to the front and lightly tapped her back with the flat of his hand.

Brie heard Marquis command his sub, "Hold her hands."

She felt Celestia lean against the opposite side of the ottoman and take Brie's cold hands in her warm ones. The connection was instantly comforting.

Marquis spoke to Brie in a soothing voice. "You will listen to the music as you embrace the caress of the flogger. Let it remind you of your power. Be confident and *know* that circumstances cannot diminish your strength. Nothing can."

Brie nodded.

"Are you ready, pearl?"

"Yes, Master."

Mozart filled the room as he warmed up her skin with light hits from the flogger. It took several minutes for her to relax but as soon as she did, he leaned in and asked her color.

"Green."

He shifted his stance and brought more strength to each swing. Brie moaned as the endorphins flowed and her limbs began to tingle, but she begged him to increase the strength of his hits.

"I am not your pain addiction," he reprimanded. "You take what I give you."

She felt ashamed, knowing he'd rightly perceived her desire to escape through pain.

"I will leave no marks for your Master, pearl. Fully appreciate each contact against your skin and you will not need it stronger," he instructed. "I give this to you as empowerment, not escape."

Celestia squeezed her hands in encouragement. Brie took a deep breath and rolled her shoulders before straightening her back for more. She received the next stroke with a different mindset. It sent shivers of electricity through her. She harnessed it.

Each successive stroke increased her resolve. *I am powerful. I choose my submission… I choose whom I will serve.*

She wanted to protest when he stopped, but realized their time was running short. The music ended and he removed the blindfold. "Better?"

Brie nodded. "Yes. Thank you, Master."

He took her hand and helped her up. He nodded to Celestia, who moved gracefully to the bed in the corner of the room and lay down. Marquis Gray guided Brie to it and commanded her to lie beside his sub. He joined them on the bed, sandwiching Brie between them. It was comforting on a level she hadn't experienced before.

"Remember that I told you not to settle for the status quo."

She shivered unwillingly and felt both bodies press against her. Brie whispered, "I will miss you, Marquis Gray."

"You have been an experience, pearl."

Celestia spoke up, her voice pure, like spring rain. "I've been interested in your progress ever since I heard about your near-dismissal, Miss Bennett."

Brie remembered that night clearly. The panel had suggested Sir step down as headmaster and she had almost been kicked out of the submissive program altogether.

Marquis' laugh was low and heartfelt. "I saw your strength even then. I knew you would survive the taint of Thane's interference."

"Taint?" Brie questioned.

"Admit that you have been influenced by that one private encounter."

Brie shook her head. "I was influenced the day Sir came into the tobacco shop."

Marquis Gray snorted. "Still, he used his position to take something that was not his to possess."

"Marquis Gray, I wanted no other."

He shook his head angrily. "You were his student. It was unconscionable."

"Still...I do not regret it."

"Your defense of the act does not negate the transgression. Coen wanted both of you out. If it hadn't been for Gallant's unwavering belief in you, you would not be here."

"I never understood Master Coen's aversion to me."

Marquis corrected her. "Coen would do anything to protect the sanctity of the program. The fact you eventually earned his respect speaks volumes."

Brie braved a question she had been wanting to ask. "Why does Ms. Clark hate me?"

"Hate is a strong word."

Celestia answered her. "You act as a whetting stone for Mistress Clark."

Marquis reached over Brie and stroked his submissive's cheek. "True enough, love."

Brie's heart warmed at the term of endearment coming from the fierce trainer's lips. Their relationship was exactly what she desired for herself.

"You unbalance our normally controlled Dominatrix. Although it was entertaining to watch, Coen was right to be concerned and we set things in place to limit your exposure to each other. Every trainer comes across a student they cannot instruct. It happens."

"Then why was I partnered with her this last time?"

"Thane did not want you to leave the school with a negative impression of Dommes. He asked Clark to repair any damage she had done. You should know she willingly agreed."

"Well, I was almost convinced her feelings towards me had changed."

"Do not dwell on it."

Brie looked around the room and said wistfully, "I will really miss this place."

"The Center is only a stepping stone, pearl. Your true destiny lies beyond. Don't look back."

She frowned when she thought of Faelan next door

and Tono off somewhere, talking to his father.

Marquis grabbed her chin, focusing her attention back on him. "You seem confused by the unexpected turn of events tonight, but your decision remains the same."

She looked into his dark eyes and disagreed. "That's not true. I don't know what to do now."

He shook his head, but was slow to elaborate. "You have already decided. I saw it in your eyes earlier. You simply haven't accepted it yet."

He sounded so confident that Brie believed him. "How is it you understand me better than I do myself? You always have."

"Men are driven by sex to understand the feminine mind. Not by money, career or recognition."

His words were profound and resonated through her. She finally understood her attraction to D/s. The unique sexual relationship was conducive to a deeper connection between a man and woman. A connection not found elsewhere.

The bell rang with its ten minute warning. Marquis had her stand as Celestia covered her back in soothing lotion before placing her corset back on and tying it tightly. Brie realized he had been gentle in his flogging so that it did not hurt overly much. He'd thought of everything—he always had.

Celestia brushed out her hair and touched up her makeup in the few remaining minutes. "I want you to be perfect for your Master," she said, smiling like a proud mother.

My Master…

Marquis guided the two of them out of the room and Brie ran smack into Mary. Faelan was nowhere to be seen.

"What the hell, Mary?" Brie hissed.

"You're the one who taught me to follow my heart," she answered defensively. "Besides, if I don't look out for myself, who will?"

"But *Faelan?*" Brie growled.

"Yes, Faelan." Mary turned away from her and whispered something to Master Coen before disappearing back into the room.

Brie was about to scream the word 'bitch' when she noticed Tono out of the corner of her eye. She could barely control her joy and eagerly motioned him into the room. Marquis nodded his agreement and gestured for Tono to join Brie. The smile on his beautiful face chased away all her ugly thoughts.

"You came back," she said, trying not to sound as relieved as she felt.

"Of course, toriko. I would never leave you for long."

She blushed at the thrill his words brought. The instant the door closed, he grabbed her and pulled her into his arms. He shut his eyes and simply held her. She could sense his distress and trembled in the embrace.

Tono responded to her fear by pressing her head against his chest, holding her tighter. She accepted the constriction and breathed with him, standing in silence as she soaked in their simple harmony.

Brie eventually pulled away, knowing that she only had a limited time. "Tono…" She took his hand and tried to lead him to the couch. Instead, he directed her to the mat.

"Present yourself to me, little slave."

Brie obediently dropped to the floor and arched her back in a beautiful curved shape, with her legs spread wide for his pleasure, just as he had instructed her in their first session together. She kept her head down, waiting for his next order.

Tono fisted her hair, pulling her head back and kissing her deeply. "My toriko, how well you remember my preference."

"I delight in pleasing you, Tono."

He smiled as he gracefully knelt down on the mat, gesturing her to him. Tono wrapped his strong arms around Brie and she laid her head back on his chest. She wanted to voice the question that was burning a hole in her heart but she chickened out, choosing instead to ask the first question from her list. "Can you tell me how old you are?"

He smiled and kissed the top of her head. "I am thirty."

She quickly did the math and announced, "You're only eight years older. That's not bad."

"Glad you approve, little one."

She giggled softly. "I already know what you do for a living…so I guess I'll go on to the next question. Why did you choose to become a Dom?"

"My father is a master of Kinbaku. It seemed only natural that I should follow in his footsteps. You see, I have been trained by the best."

The mention of his father threw Brie off, so she

changed the subject. "What do you think of my film career?"

"I will support you fully, toriko. I have the unique ability to travel with you on location, no matter where you end up shooting. I can continue my photography and do seminars anywhere. Your career choice is not an issue for me."

"But I thought you liked to stay in LA?"

"It is my preference, but not a necessity. I would enjoy seeing you succeed in your passion, and I desire to support you."

She grabbed his cheeks and kissed him soundly. "It means a lot to me, Tono. More than you know."

"I know your heart, little one."

"So I assume we would be together twenty-four seven."

He ran his fingertips down her neck and over the swell of her breasts. "I would have it no other way."

"Your place?" she asked, with a touch of sarcastic acceptance.

"It matters little." She looked at him in surprise. He answered her next question without being asked. "My contentment is not dependent on the location."

Brie smiled, liking all of his answers so far. "Would you have a problem with me working at the tobacco shop until I get my big break?"

He surprised her when he said, "Yes."

She was about to argue the point, but he caressed her cheek lovingly. "You should not work a retail job, toriko, when your career involves film. I expect you to devote your time fully to it."

Brie broke out in a huge grin. "You would support me until I make it a success?"

"Of course, little slave. Your success is our success. However, I would require your beautiful form on my own film occasionally."

She knocked him over with her enthusiastic embrace. They landed on the mat together, her laughter filling the small room. "I love you so much!"

Once the L-word was out, the room became silent. He slowly brushed a strand of hair from her face, looking at her with those warm, brown eyes. He said nothing, but his smile was radiant, like the sun. It thrilled her heart to see it.

Tono gently helped her up. He stood before her, taking off his jacket and laying it neatly on the floor. Then he proceeded to undress in front of her. She watched in admiration as he exposed his model-worthy body. When he was completely nude, he picked up his jacket and pulled a small piece of jute from a pocket. "Hold your wrists out, toriko."

Brie struggled to hide her grin. The rope was so short. How could he possibly do anything impressive with such a small piece of rope? Tono's eyes sparkled as he secured her wrists together in a cross pattern, leaving her arms open. He pushed her gently onto the mat and removed her thong first. He kissed it before placing it on the floor. He removed her heels next, slowly and reverently. Her stockings came off last.

Tono flipped her microskirt up and stroked her bare pussy. Brie's body responded, automatically pressing against his hand, desiring more of his intimate touch.

"So beautiful," he murmured. Instead of claiming her with his tongue, Tono stood and pulled Brie up. He leaned over and lifted her tied wrists over his head. With her arms around his neck and her face just inches from his, he picked her up. She automatically wrapped her legs around his naked hips and felt the sexual tension when her swollen lips made contact with his hard cock.

Tono danced with her in his arms, kissing her deeply as he kept time to a song only he could hear. His tongue drew her in like an undercurrent. She lost herself in the kiss, no longer aware of her surroundings.

Her pussy gently rocked against his shaft as he moved, causing a slow buildup that accented the song he created between them. "Oh, Tono," she whispered.

He lifted her hips up and slowly slipped his cock into her. She threw her head back and cried out in ecstasy. He continued to dance with her, his cock planted deeply within.

Brie pulled on her bound wrists, drawing his lips back to hers. He moved in a circular pattern around the room, sliding himself in and out of her moist recess. Her building orgasm was approaching its peak. Brie braced her wrists against the back of his neck and rubbed her erect nipples against his sweaty skin. It proved his undoing and she felt his cock pulse rhythmically inside her as he groaned hoarsely.

The constant rubbing had sensitized her clit to near climax. She whispered, "Bite me, Tono," needing his teeth to bring her over the edge.

He hesitated. "No."

Tono chose to give her a passionate kiss. Brie readjusted and concentrated on the magic of his tongue. Soon her body shuddered in its own release. He continued to hold her in his arms afterwards, as they basked in the afterglow of their lovemaking.

Brie winced when the warning bell rang. She hated to break the spell, but time was running out and they had to talk about his father. "Tono…" She stopped, her heart pounding with dread as a deathlike silence filled the room.

Finally, he spoke. "Toriko, my father is mistaken."

She stiffened in his embrace. "What does he mean by telling you I'm not good?" she asked, tears blurring her vision of his face.

Tono leaned forward and kissed them away. "He does not understand. My father has never shared the connection we share."

"But what did he mean by it?"

Tono closed his eyes and did not speak. It scared her. When he opened his chocolate eyes again he said firmly, "What he says does not matter."

"But it matters to me," she insisted.

He moved over to the couch and set her down, then began untying the jute. "My father believes you have a ravenous spirit."

Ice crystals coursed through her veins at the declaration. "What does that mean, Tono?"

He gazed into her eyes and paused before answering. "He does not believe I will be enough for you."

Her heart skipped a beat at hearing her greatest fear voiced by his father. Tears threatened to take over, so she squeezed her eyes tightly shut.

"My father is wrong, toriko," he said soothingly. He was tender as he dressed her.

Brie opened her eyes to stare at her handsome Dom while he dressed himself, wondering the whole time how they could survive his father's disapproval. The Japanese culture placed a high value on the bond between parent and child. Worse was the fact that Tono's father had also trained him. It demanded an even higher level of respect. But what really scared Brie—what made it difficult for her to breathe—was the fact his father might be right, and Tono and Brie both knew it.

She stood up and clung to Tono, flinching when the second bell sounded. She struggled to let go of him.

Tono took her face in his hands. "Do not let my father's words sway you, toriko. Choose the man who will love and guide you."

Marquis entered the room and encouraged Tono to leave. Brie watched him walk away, heartsick at the separation.

"Do you have what you need to make a decision, pearl?"

She looked up at Marquis and answered with a simple nod.

"Good."

They walked out of the room to the festivities now in full swing. It would be a full hour before the collaring ceremony. Brie saw Lea already mingling with the crowd. She looked over the sea of people and noticed several familiar faces.

I guess it's time to begin my goodbyes... Brie thought.

She approached Baron first. He was engaged in a

conversation with Mr. Gallant, but ended it as soon as he noticed her. "Ah, kitten…"

She grinned at the striking Dom. "I want to thank you, Baron."

His white teeth gleamed against his dark skin. "It was my pleasure and honor."

Brie smiled shyly when she admitted, "Remember that first night? I was so scared of you."

His large thumb traced the edge of her bottom lip. "It concerned me, but we got past that."

"You were gentle and kind."

He chuckled in his deep baritone. "Not too gentle, I trust."

She kissed his thumb. "Just right."

"Thankfully, Headmaster Davis picked the best man for the job." He thrust his chest out and smiled heroically. "He insisted I push you to the edge that first night, but you handled yourself well and I must say you have blossomed since, kitten. You are a true submissive now."

She stood on her tiptoes to kiss Baron's enticing, thick lips. "I owe my success to you. You saw me through that first night."

"No, you succeeded all on your own, kitten. Although I must admit it was enjoyable being a part of your training."

Mr. Gallant interrupted their conversation. "Pardon me, Miss Bennett, but there are quite a few people who would like to speak with you tonight. I recommend you spread yourself around as much as possible."

She bowed to her teacher and his beautiful wife, giving Baron one last peck on his luscious lips before moving into the crowd. Brie did a double-take when she saw her boss, Mr. Reynolds, from the tobacco shop. *What is he doing here?*

His wrinkled face broke out in a familiar grin as she came up to him. "Brie, you look positively stunning."

She was suddenly reminded of her attire and blushed. This was Mr. Reynolds, after all. "This is my wife, Judy. She has been anxious to meet you."

Brie looked at the older woman, who had streaks of gray throughout her jet-black hair. The woman had a captivating smile. "Such a pleasure. Jack has only nice things to say about his favorite employee." She leaned in closer. "I think you saved his sanity on numerous occasions."

She looked back at Mr. Reynolds, wondering at his presence here, but she didn't have to wonder for long. "I know it must be a shock to see me, but I have known Thane for a very long time. Since he was a baby, in fact." He pointed at Sir across the room. "You see, he's my nephew."

Brie gasped. Mr. Reynolds was related to Sir? She stared at Mr. Reynolds and nodded stupidly as she tried to take in his words.

"That night you met, he was actually coming by to visit me. Apparently, he was so taken by a certain young lady that he up and left without even saying hello. I have to admit I was shocked he left the card, and even more so when I saw you wearing his collar."

Mr. Reynolds knew what was going on the entire time?

"Thane's either at work or over at the Center. I had high hopes when I saw the collar around your neck, but I should have known better." He laughed lightly and held up his glass in a mock toast to Sir. "Always the bridesmaid, never the bride."

Brie's gaze gravitated towards Sir. He was smiling at some remark Master Coen had made, but his smile made her sad. Sir had poured everything into the Submissive Training Center. Lea, Mary and she were all products of his dedication and would move on from the school, partnered with Doms worthy of their new training. He, however, would remain behind—alone.

"So, Miss Bennett, have you decided who you are going to ask to collar you?" Mrs. Reynolds asked excitedly.

"Judy! You don't ask something like that," Mr. Reynolds scolded, putting his arm around his wife's shoulders. "We don't get out much. Please forgive her enthusiasm."

"That's okay," Brie replied, but she began looking around for a means of escape. She saw Faelan standing a short distance away, obviously wanting to talk to her. She made her excuse to the couple. "I'm sorry, there's someone I must speak to."

Faelan's blue eyes were trained on her. She walked away, listening to Mrs. Reynolds' profuse apologies, feeling the weight of Faelan's stare as she approached. Brie kept her eyes down, unsure how to begin.

"It changes nothing," he declared, lifting her chin up to look into her eyes.

"What did you do with her?"

He shook his head. "That is privileged information, blossom. It would be uncouth to speak of our encounter."

"I didn't care for it," she said simply, turning her head from him.

"It couldn't be helped," he answered, forcing her to look him in the eye.

"Do you want Mary?"

His reply was quick. "She's a beautiful girl." His answer did not please Brie and he knew it. "Blossom, it is you I want to collar. I have wanted nothing more since that night on the beach when I discovered what you are. Do not doubt that."

She glanced over and saw Mary watching their exchange. "Excuse me. I need to talk to that woman."

Brie left Faelan standing there and headed straight towards Mary. The woman stiffened visibly, and Brie watched her transform into her nemesis of old.

"What?" Mary growled. "I told you I wanted my chance with him. I never hid my intentions from you, bitch."

"You know I am considering Faelan as my Master."

"Which is exactly *why* I had to make my move tonight."

The look in Mary's eyes was something new. There was a look of vulnerability underneath all the bravado. Brie didn't need her to complicate matters further. "Stay far from him," she snapped, then walked away before she said something cruel.

Lea caught up with Brie. "What's going on?"

"Do you know what Mary did?"

"Yeah. I can't believe she would go after Faelan like that. What did he say to you afterwards?"

Brie sighed. "Well, he claims I'm the only one he wants to collar, but he admits he has the hots for the cow."

"What about Tono? What happened with him?"

Brie rolled her eyes in an attempt to keep the tears from forming. "Oh, his dad thinks I'm no good."

"That's bullshit!" Lea blurted loudly. Several groups of people turned towards them and Lea clamped her hands over her mouth. "I'm sorry, Brie," she whispered, "but I just can't believe that. You are the best sub to graduate from this place. How can he say that?"

Brie struggled to say the words that rang in her head. "He says I have a ravenous soul…"

Lea wrapped Brie in her arms and pressed her against those very large breasts. "No! Don't even go there. You have a beautiful soul and Tono is lucky to love you."

Brie buried her head in Lea's chest, suddenly feeling like a little kid. "I love him, Lea. I do, but…"

"But what, sweetie?" she asked, moving Brie's hair out of the way so she could hear her better.

Brie said in the barest of whispers, "I don't know if our love will be enough."

Lea squeezed her then, long and hard. Brie could feel the blood pounding in her head from the lack of oxygen, but she didn't move from her friend's embrace until Lea let go. She held Brie by her shoulders and smiled. "What did the sadistic Dom say to his helplessly bound sub as he cut at her bonds with a machete?"

Brie shrugged, struggling to participate in Lea's poor attempt at distraction.

Lea answered with a huge grin, "Tonight, we're going

vanilla!"

Brie shook her head at the terrible joke, but let a weak smile make its way to her face. Lea was always good for a laugh. "I'm going to miss you, girl."

Lea protested. "Oh, no, you're not getting rid of me that easy. Sorry, Stinky Cheese, you are stuck with me for life."

Brie gave her an overenthusiastic hip bump that set her off balance. Lea was just about to return the favor when her face went slack and her jaw dropped.

"*Radost moya.*"

That deep sound reverberated through Brie and she turned slowly towards his voice. Rytsar Durov stood before her in all his Russian glory. She suddenly felt shy standing before the impressive Dom. Brie quickly looked to the floor and tried to calm her erratic pulse as she bowed before him.

Brie snuck a peek, and then smiled when she saw the mischievous glint in his eye. "My warrior returns," she whispered.

His low rolling laughter filled the entire commons. "*Radost moya* has grown up, I see." He lifted Brie off the ground and crushed her to his chest. She'd forgotten how strong and muscular he was.

She wasn't sure how to act, now that she knew he was a prominent Dom in Europe. It was as intimidating as she'd thought it would be. Brie looked up at him shyly, "It seems you speak English."

He winked as he lifted her higher and kissed her hard on the lips. She was instantly transported back to her warrior fantasy, where he had fulfilled her every desire. It left her shaky and weak.

Rytsar placed her back on the ground and motioned to one of his entourage. The beefy bodyguard produced a package and handed it to Rytsar, who in turn handed it to Brie.

"This is for you, my little joy. In honor of your graduation."

Brie slowly unwrapped the gold paper and lifted the lid of the box. Inside was an exquisite set of golden handcuffs encrusted with small jewels. She touched the multicolored stones in admiration. "Thank you, Rytsar. It's stunning."

"Something useful your Master might enjoy." He looked up and motioned Sir over, then slapped him heartily on the back. "I cannot stay, *moy droog*. However, I wanted to congratulate you on training such a rare beauty. If she could handle Russian winters I would claim her for my own."

Sir looked genuinely pleased when he answered Rytsar. "I am glad you came, Durov, although I am disappointed that you cannot stay. We should get together and catch up."

"Yes. Drag your sorry *zhopa* out of this school for a couple of weeks and join me in Russia. I promise to show you a grandiose time." He raised his hands in the air, spreading his arms wide.

Sir's laughter warmed Brie's heart. "Yes, well, some of us have to work for a living."

Rytsar growled loudly. "Peasant."

Sir answered in mock disgust, "Aristocrat."

The muscular Russian laughed as he smacked Sir

hard on the back again. "Come join me later tonight. You know where." He turned his attention back to Brie. He took her hand and turned it palm up before planting a sensual kiss in the center. "Choose wisely, *radost moya*."

With that, he left with Sir, who escorted the entire entourage out—the impressive Rytsar and his three beefy bodyguards. When they were out of earshot, Lea whispered appreciatively, "Damn…"

"Yeah," Brie replied.

Lea asked to look at Rytsar's gift and dug the hand-cuffs out of the box, holding them up for a better look. "Girl, he couldn't have come up with a better gift for a sub who likes bondage."

"Yeah, yeah, put it back," Brie ordered, feeling embarrassed by the expensive gift.

"Oh, no, you have to wear this. It's far too pretty to keep inside a box." Lea took the key attached to the cuffs and opened one up, looping it around the chain on Brie's waist. She stood back to admire her work. "Yes, now you are utterly irresistible."

Brie looked down and swung her hips, listening to the pleasant jingle of the cuffs. It did look like a lovely accent piece. She looked up to thank Lea, but saw that her friend had moved over to talk to the Sheik and his five comely harem girls.

Rachael Dunningham took the opportunity to step over and talk to Brie. "Hello, Miss Bennett. I want to let you know what a pleasure it has been to work with you."

"No, thank you, Rachael. It was your helpfulness and professionalism that convinced me this school was legit. If it weren't for you, I never would have enrolled."

"Speaking about enrollment, you might be happy to learn that the young lady you emailed about has contacted the school. Candy Moore will be starting the next session in two weeks."

Brie was thrilled by the news. "Rachael, that's absolutely wonderful! I've worried about her ever since that day on the bus." She gave Rachael a big hug, and then another for good measure. "I'll start payments next week."

Rachael smiled amiably. "No need. She has procured a sponsor."

Brie leaned in close. "Can I ask who?"

"Normally, we don't divulge such information. However, you have a vested interest in the girl so I don't see any harm. Mr. Gallant is paying her tuition."

Brie glanced over to where Mr. Gallant stood with his arm around the waist of his submissive wife. *What an extraordinary man.*

"Please do not let him know I told you. He's an excruciatingly humble person," Rachael warned.

"Duly noted," Brie answered, but she couldn't help staring at the short yet imposing Dom. She had always admired her teacher, but Mr. Gallant truly was a man above all men.

Marquis Gray motioned Brie over and announced, "It is almost time. Are you ready?"

Brie nodded, confident in her decision. Of the two men, she knew whom she wanted to serve, despite her reservations.

Marquis guided her to a separate room that held a small, round table. The table was elegantly dressed in red velvet with an exquisite collar in the center. The silver piece was delicately engraved. Brie lightly touched the pearl that hung in front. Even more enchanting was the heart-shaped lock that fastened in the back. Beside it lay an intricate key on a chain. The key would be worn by her Master.

"You will wait here until your name is announced. Stand beside Headmaster Davis and he will speak a few words to the community. Once he gives you permission, you will walk up to the Dom of your choice and kneel before him, holding up the collar and key. If he accepts your offer, a formal Collaring Ceremony will begin. During the ceremony, you will give your vows to one another and your Master will place the collar around your neck, accepting you as his submissive."

Brie felt the butterflies start just listening to his instructions. In a few minutes, she would be kneeling before her Master. She took a couple of deep breaths to calm her nerves and then smiled at Marquis Gray. "This is it."

"Yes, pearl. Your time has come. Embrace it with courage and don't look back."

"I will…Master."

He gave her a crooked smile. "Master to you no longer."

She heard Sir's strong voice outside the room. "As a graduate, each submissive is given the opportunity to partake in the Collaring Ceremony. This year, one submissive has chosen to do so. Miss Bennett, present yourself to the community."

Marquis offered his arm and escorted her out. She

made her way to Sir with her eyes downcast and her poor heart beating like a snare drum. Once she was at his side, she knelt down, facing the community, and waited for him to begin.

"As is tradition for our school, a submissive who feels she has found her Master at the end of the course is allowed to present a ceremonial collar to the Dom of her choice. If accepted, a formal collaring ceremony will immediately follow."

Sir turned and looked down at Brie. "Such a union is not to be entered into lightly. Are you secure in your decision?"

She glanced up at him and nodded. "I am, Sir."

He then commanded in an official tone, "Miss Bennett, present your collar now."

Brie gracefully rocked off her heels and stood up, looking at Tono and Faelan on the other side of the room. The men stood side by side, but both only had eyes for her. She held herself erect as she started towards her Master. She walked fluidly and with confidence, just as she had been taught.

Brie peeked at Tono. He was smiling, peace and assurance flowing from him like a river. Beside him stood his father. The small man was also staring at her, but his mouth was a hard line, his disapproval easy to read.

She glanced at Faelan. He was gazing at her intently, a half-grin gracing his handsome face. Brie caught a glimpse of Mary behind him and saw a look of complete devastation. It made her stop in her tracks.

Brie could feel the tension rise in the room.

Time slowed down to a crawl as everything suddenly

came into focus. As much as she loved Tono, he would not be able to meet her deepest desires. Faelan shared those same desires, but she did not love him. Brie knew what she wanted beyond a shadow of a doubt. There was no other choice—there never had been.

She turned around and walked towards Sir, the delicate collar held out before her. She saw the slight shake of his head but she ignored it.

Brie knelt down at his feet and held the collar and key up to him. Silence filled the huge room. She patiently waited for Sir to take them from her. As the seconds dragged by, however, a cold chill entered her heart.

He finally spoke a soft but commanding, "No."

Brie shuddered in disbelief, her heart crushing in on itself as she remained bowed before him. He had warned her that this would happen... *This is my fault.* Now the entire room knew her choice and there was no turning back.

Tears fell as she slowly stood up and turned from him. Her feet made their way to the exit as if of their own accord. No one spoke as the crowd silently parted in front of her.

She would scream later, in the privacy of her own pain. Right now, her only goal was to make it out of the Center with what little dignity she had left. She lifted her head, even though she could not see through the tears. *Don't run, Brie. Walk...*

Brie Bows Before *Him*

Before she could make it to the elevator, his voice floated over the sea of people. "Brie."

She pressed the button, unsure if it was her own wishful thinking.

"Come back and face me."

Brie inhaled deeply before turning around. She wiped the tears away and looked Sir straight in the eye as she hesitantly made her way back to him. His eyes conveyed nothing—neither hope nor disapproval.

"Kneel."

It took all of her will to kneel before him again. She felt his hand on her head and gasped at the warmth that flowed into her soul. He announced in a voice that encompassed the entire room, "I resign as headmaster of the school."

Brie could feel the shockwave ripple through the multitudes.

"I offer up Master Anderson as a worthy replacement, but the panel will be in charge of the final decision."

The room remained hushed.

"Offer your collar to me again," Sir commanded. She held her breath as he took the collar and key she held out to him. "I accept this collar as a symbol of the offering of yourself, and promise to thoughtfully guide and lead you."

A chime sounded, marking the beginning of the formal ceremony.

Breathe, Brie, breathe…

He knelt beside her, stating, "You belong to me from this day onward. I will do all within my power to protect and keep you as you join me on this journey."

Her lips trembled as she felt the hands of her Master fasten the collar around her neck and click the lock into place.

Sir stood back up. "You will wear this symbol of my ownership as a sign of our commitment to one another."

Brie's voice shook as she made her vow to him. "I accept this symbol of your ownership and will wear it proudly for all to see, Sir."

"And I shall wear this key as a symbol of our commitment," he said, placing it around his neck. His next announcement filled the room. "You now belong to me."

Brie felt the heat rise in the core of her being at his declaration. "I now belong to you, Master," she agreed breathlessly.

"I accept your request to serve me and will honor your needs and desires. Trust that I will always put your best interests foremost in my dominance over you. Your happiness, health and well-being are in my care, and I will consciously tend to them because you are a part of me."

A part of you... "Sir, I will honor and love you as I serve you to the best of my ability. My submission to you is freely given. I am now a part of you and will respect your dominance over me as our lives become one." She leaned forward and kissed both of his feet as a gesture of her submission.

"Stand before your Master."

Brie stood up, quivering with joy. Sir lifted her chin and kissed her in front of the crowd, to seal their commitment. The entire room broke out in applause as the chime rang out three times to end the ceremony.

As the last ring dissipated, Sir lifted her off the ground in a flurry of motion, cradling her against his chest. He walked towards his office, announcing to the other trainers as he passed, "I will be clearing out my things."

Brie was unaware of anything but his masculine scent as she buried her face in his chest. That, and the sound of his confident stride echoing through the hallway. He did not speak as he opened the office door, carried her in, then locked it behind him.

Sir swept the items off his desk with one hand as he held her with the other. Then he gently set her down upon it. "Do you realize what you've just done?"

She looked up at him lovingly. "I could not deny my heart, Sir." Then she added, "But I did not mean for you to resign from the Center."

"There was no other option. Surely you understood that."

She closed her eyes in guilty admission. "I did not think that far ahead."

He chuckled softly. "No, you wouldn't. You run on instinct—you always have."

She braved his steady gaze, afraid to voice her next question but determined to ask. "Do your regret your decision?"

"Regret?" He rubbed his chin, seemingly giving thought to the question before answering. "Regret is not something I do. However, I am surprised to find myself in this predicament." He looked at her accusingly. "For a submissive, you've never quite grasped the idea of following orders."

She blushed, unable to defend herself.

"Mercifully, your disobedience was exactly what I required."

Sir glanced around the room at the numerous bookshelves of leather-bound books, mementos, and pictures. Then he gazed down at her with a possessive smirk that melted her heart. "Mine."

"All yours, Sir."

She cried out in need when he grasped the back of her neck and pressed his lips against hers. *My Master's lips…*

The contact sent her on a sub high all its own. His love, mixed with his dominance, was something she hadn't experienced with Sir before.

He broke away from her and said huskily, "You cannot know the number of times I sat in this office, imagining what I would do if I had you all to myself." He looked around. "Since this will no longer be mine once I leave, I think we should indulge my fantasies."

"Your will is my pleasure," she answered breathlessly.

He pulled on the key attached to her golden cuffs, breaking the string that held it. Then he undid the lock and unhooked the cuffs from her belt. "Time to break these in."

Brie held out her arms to her Master and watched him tighten the cuffs around her wrists. Although they were made of metal, they had been crafted with rounded corners so they did not cut into her skin. The clicking sound as they locked into place made her wet. He must have sensed it because he slipped his hand between her legs, stroking her clit with his thumb. She moaned in appreciation, loving the feel of Sir's touch.

He looked towards the ceiling and then lifted her off the desk. Holding her arms above her head, he secured the cuffs to a small hook attached to the ceiling—one she had never noticed before. It left her almost tiptoeing in a lean, beautiful pose. His hands traveled down the curves of her body as he whistled appreciatively.

"I've always found your body irresistible, Brie. From that very first meeting in the tobacco shop I knew I wanted to possess it... You."

She whimpered when his mouth claimed her again. He was so totally male, completely enveloping her spirit. Sir pulled back and retrieved an item from his desk. It turned out to be a box cutter. She watched in fearful fascination as he meticulously cut each tie of her expensive corset and let it fall to the ground.

"Better," he complimented as he cupped her breasts

in his strong hands. He then removed the intricate arm bracelet and tossed it in the trash. Her long, brown curls tumbled down as the wolf comb found its home in the trash bin next to the dragon.

His hands traveled farther down, removing her tight-fitting skirt and thong. "You've always looked good in just hose and heels, babygirl." She felt his warm breath on her neck and her nipples became hard as she anticipated his teeth on her skin.

"You smell of other men. I must remedy that." Sir exited the room and quickly returned with a washcloth and a bowl of warm, soapy water. He washed every inch of her exposed skin with citrus bubbles, including the area between her legs. He left her again, then returned with fresh water. Once he'd made Brie pure for him, Sir began nibbling on her neck.

Brie's knees would have buckled if she hadn't been held up by her restraints. His teeth grazed her skin down the center of her chest. He stopped to gently nip her breasts before heading down her stomach, making his way to her bare pussy. Sir grabbed her ass in both hands and dragged his tongue over her swollen lips. "Fuck, you taste good." He separated her outer lips and took another long lick. She groaned as she twisted on the hook.

Sir smiled and stood up, then moved over to his desk to sit down. "I imagined you just like this, bound to be used at my disposal. To taste at my leisure." He picked up a box of books from the floor and dumped them out. Then he began the task of clearing out his office, starting with his desk.

It was distressing to see Sir emptying the office of his belongings, but whenever he looked at her she experienced an electric jolt, feeling only gratitude that he had given up his position for her. After several minutes, he put down the box and approached her again with a strip of cloth in his hand.

He tied it over her eyes, murmuring, "Ah, the allure of the unknown. Where will I touch you?"

She inhaled as his fingertips lightly traced the contours of her arm. She giggled and flinched when he reached her armpit. When his hand fell away, she instantly regretted her reaction and hoped he would return.

His fingertips resumed their teasing, trailing down the other arm. She moaned, enjoying the tickling fire of his touch as the sensations traveled to her groin. "I love you, Sir," she whispered.

She felt his hot breath next to her ear. "What did you say?"

"I love you."

His mouth landed on hers as he crushed her in a tight embrace, but then he moved away and she heard him throwing more items into his box. The exchange left her disconcerted. He hadn't returned her words of affection. Goose bumps rose on her skin at the thought he might not love her, and a soft whimper escaped her lips.

She felt him return to her side. His fingers traced her jawline and lightly grazed her trembling lower lip. "The day I took your anal virginity, I'd never felt so vulnerable yet so powerful in my life. I fell in love with you then, and have only suffered for it ever since."

She whispered, "Suffer no more." The only thing she wanted at that moment was to feel his love inside her.

"Are you suggesting I take you, Brie?" He moved away and went back to packing. She heard him haphazardly throwing items into the box. It seemed so unlike his neat and orderly persona. She realized she was the reason—it was an intoxicating power to have over Sir.

He spoke as she listened to him rummage through his bookcase. "I always told myself that the second I stopped caring about the Training Center, I would resign. When I saw you walking away from me, I knew that moment had come. The bravery it took to defy protocol and risk everything was inspiring, babygirl."

His words touched the core of her, the same way his touch invaded her skin.

"I have avoided you for so long, it seems like a sin to partake of you now." He paused and added in a sultry voice, "Fortunately, your Master enjoys sinful pleasures."

He unhooked Brie from the cuffs, removed the blindfold, and laid her on the carpeted floor. He joined her after relieving himself of his clothes. She worshipped his masculine chest and princely cock framed in dark hair.

Sir's hand trailed over her skin as he spoke. "All this time wanting to slip into your womanhood, but having to watch others enjoy it."

She looked at him questioningly. "Why couldn't you have taken me, Master?"

He traced her lips with his index finger. "I knew if I ever allowed myself the luxury, I would be utterly lost."

"You were, regardless."

His eyes narrowed. "At least I had the illusion of control." Sir kissed her then, without restraint. All the love, passion, and lust communicated itself through his lips. Brie met the kiss, equally desperate to express the pent-up feelings she'd been forced to hold back for so long.

They bruised each other in their violent embrace, releasing a torrent of emotion. "Babygirl…" His hands grabbed, clawed, and pressed her against him. He was a man ravenous for what was now his, and she gave herself over to his need, reveling in her Master's fierce desire.

Her Master's body nearly crushed her as he lay on top of her small frame, his tongue plundering her willing mouth. She fully expected his taking of her to be equally wild, but he stopped himself.

"No."

She was sure he'd said it to himself. Sir's lustful gaze softened and she saw the hint of love behind it. The love she had longed to see, fully reflected in his eyes.

He looked down at her as if she were his princess, his treasure. "So breathtaking." He spread her legs apart and settled in between them. "This will not be fast, babygirl. I will take you excruciatingly, tortuously slow. I've waited too long to rush."

He pressed the head of his cock against her opening. She tried to grab his buttocks, but he commanded, "Lie perfectly still. I want you to fully experience and remember the first time you were taken by your Master."

Brie lay back, her heart racing at the thought. He

kissed her breasts as his cock slowly pushed against her and then breached the entrance. She gasped in pleasure.

Master was inside her…

His lips moved up to her neck as his shaft made its way farther in. Tears pooled in her eyes as his princely cock filled her mind, body, and soul. There was nothing more she wanted, nothing more she needed.

His mouth found hers again as he made his final push into her depths. They both cried out at the connection.

"May I, Master?" she whispered.

When he nodded, she wrapped her arms and legs around him. Sir grabbed her face and kissed her fiercely as he began stroking her with his shaft. Brie moaned in ecstasy. Nothing she'd experienced compared to this— *nothing.*

His thrusting came faster and faster as he gave in to his lust. She met him stroke for stroke, forcing him into her as deeply as her body would allow. "My Sir…"

He put his hand under the small of her back, tilting her hips more severely so that he could reach deeper inside her. She screamed out in pleasure as his cock claimed all of her. He fucked her, then—hard, deep, and without pity. She took it joyously, never wanting it to end, but then he commanded, "Come for your Master."

"Yes…oh, yes!"

The instant his cock began its deep shuddering, Brie's body responded by squeezing hard, caressing his manhood with her own intense orgasm. Reality blurred as she lost herself in him. Sir bit her neck as he shot his seed deep inside her, his love bursting throughout her entire body.

I have never known such bliss…

When he pulled away, she saw the look of vulnerability she'd seen several times before. This time, however, he did not hide it. He looked her in the eye. "You are mine, Brie Bennett. I will never let you go."

After his pronouncement, he got up off the floor and went to his desk. He pulled something out of the drawer and came back to her with an impish grin. He took the top off the permanent marker and, with fluid strokes, wrote a word on her chest. He sat back with a self-satisfied smirk. Brie looked down and saw that he had written the word *Mine* in big, flowing letters.

He handed the pen to her. She smiled shyly as she wrote on his hairy chest. He nodded his approval when he read the word: *Master*. Sir fisted her hair and drew her to him, kissing her possessively. "Never forget that."

She shook her head. "I won't, Sir… I can't."

He commanded her to re-dress as he put on his clothes. When she came to her corset, she held it up to him and pouted.

Sir grinned lustfully and took it from her, then threw the useless piece of clothing in his box. "You won't be needing it, babygirl. You already have on what I want you to wear." He nodded at her chest.

Brie looked down at his word with pride. Yes, it was enough.

He hoisted the box, grabbing the golden cuffs from the hook as he walked towards the door. Sir looked over his office one last time. "It's been a good run." He escorted her out and locked it behind him.

Sir held out his right arm and she gratefully wrapped hers around it.

"Head held high, but at a respectful angle."

"Yes, Master."

"Chest out," he commanded. Then Sir added with a captivating smirk, "Exude elegance and poise, confident in the knowledge you are mine."

Brie hid her smile as they walked back to the commons, which was still full of people. The chatter stopped and the whole room became eerily silent as the crowd turned towards the couple. Brie scanned the masses, but saw no sign of Tono. She did notice Mary standing beside Faelan. He wore a look of sheer disbelief.

Sir gave Mr. Gallant the keys. "Call if I have forgotten anything or you have questions."

"I will." Mr. Gallant looked at Brie. "Are you happy, Miss Bennett?"

"Yes, Mr. Gallant. Very much so."

"Fine. Then I wish you the best." He nodded at Sir. "Both of you."

"Thank you, Gallant," Sir replied affably, moving towards the elevator.

Marquis Gray pressed the button for them and then stood to the side. When Brie snuck a glance, he nodded at her with the slightest hint of a smile. *Did he know this would be my choice tonight?*

When the elevator doors opened, the two walked into it and turned to face the assembly. Master Anderson held up his drink and toasted Sir. "Wishing you the best, Thane. You should know that your service to the Center has been greatly appreciated."

"Hear, hear!" someone shouted.

Glasses were held up, to an enthusiastic chorus of, "To Headmaster Davis!"

The room filled with applause as the doors closed. Tears streamed down Brie's face. She was overwhelmed by how much Sir had given up to be with her.

He looked down at Brie and winked. "No need to cry, babygirl. This is just the beginning."

Her First Lesson

The large commons broke out in applause as the elevator doors closed. Brie couldn't stop the tears from falling, knowing that Sir had given up his position at the Submissive Training Center to claim her.

Her heart melted when he looked down and winked. "No need to cry, babygirl. This is just the beginning."

She smiled through the tears and slipped her hand into his. "Yes, Sir."

"No more tears," he commanded gently.

Brie dutifully wiped them away and took a deep breath. When the doors opened at the first floor, Sir put down his box of office mementoes and took off his jacket. "I can't have you walking out into the cool night like this." He wrapped his jacket, still warm from his body heat, around her naked shoulders. He buttoned it up, picked up his box again and guided her out of the elevator, saying, "Come with me, Brie."

She held her breath, loving those four simple words. Her Master was taking her *home*... She had to pinch herself to believe it.

Sir led her to the farthest corner of the parking lot, to a glossy red car that looked like it belonged in a car show, not at a community college. It was *Batman* hot.

He held out his hand and helped her into the low-lying car. She tried to enter it gracefully but fell into the bucket seat with a plop.

Sir chuckled lightly. "Such style." He slid the door closed and proceeded to the other side, then buckled himself in before starting the roaring engine.

"What kind of car is this?" she asked.

"It's not a *car*, Brie. This is a modified Lotus Evora S."

She hid her smile. Obviously, she knew nothing about his 'baby' and would need to google it later.

He drove like he played with a sub—skillfully, but pushing the limits of the vehicle. Brie flushed in excitement, knowing that Sir was taking her home to play with *her*, alone.

Brie's jaw dropped when he pulled up to the front of a towering high-rise and a debonair valet immediately ran up to greet him. Sir opened her car door, and supported Brie as she made a second attempt at being graceful upon exiting the low vehicle. She smiled and glanced up, mesmerized by the possessive look in Sir's eyes. Her heart skipped a beat when he bent down and kissed her lightly on the lips before handing over his key to the attendant.

Brie took the arm he offered her and they walked through the doors, which were held open by a doorman.

"Good evening, Mr. Davis."

Sir nodded courteously, but said nothing as he guided Brie to the elevator. The foyer of the apartment building was opulent. She couldn't imagine what his apartment must be like. She licked her lips apprehensively, feeling out of place.

"Nothing to be nervous about, babygirl," Sir said.

She whispered, "I've never been here. I feel…"

"At home," he answered for her. Her body tingled at his words.

The bell chimed and the elevator doors opened for them. Sir placed his hand on the small of her back, the electricity of his touch making her whole body quiver. The interior of the elevator was mirrored, so Brie was able to sneak glances at Sir as they traveled up to his apartment. He stared straight ahead with a slight smirk on his face, as if he was already considering what he would do with her.

Will my heart survive tonight? she wondered.

At the fifteenth floor, the door opened to a marbled hallway. Sir escorted her out and led Brie to the last door on the right. The door was made of dark wood, engraved with a symbol that looked suspiciously like a BDSM triskele, the emblem for the lifestyle. Was Sir that forthright about it? Did the whole high-rise know what he did for a living…what he *used* to do? A momentary jolt of guilt clouded her joy.

Sir opened the heavy door to a long, narrow hallway with walls covered in various forms of modern art, from sculptures mounted on the walls to alluring paintings. Brie's heels made an attractive clicking sound on the dark marble floor as he escorted her inside. The apartment smelled of Sir.

He walked her to a large, open area with windows from floor to ceiling, with a breathtaking view overlooking the city. "Impressive," she said quietly.

"I quite agree," he answered, unbuttoning the jacket he'd put around her and slipping it off her shoulders. Her nipples were already erect, begging for her Master's attention. "I prefer you like this," he murmured. His lips grazed her neck teasingly, and then he gestured towards the seating area. "Sit while I make us a drink. I would like to talk about our new arrangement."

Brie's heart fluttered as she watched him walk away. She glanced around the large room, noting that it was decorated in a minimalistic style, but the furniture was artfully placed and sensual in appearance. Sir had pointed to a black sofa, but she was drawn to an attractive red chair on the other side of the room. It was curvaceous and thin, made only for one person. She walked up to it, noting its unique shape. It was more like a chaise longue, made for a single person to lie in rather than sit. It had a high, attractively curved back and an equally aesthetic, rounded foot area. She lay down, fitting comfortably in the concave middle of the chair, and looked out over the city from her comfortable vantage point, listening to Sir moving about in the kitchen.

Brie tried to calm her nerves as she came to grips with her new reality. She was in Sir's apartment—*he* was her Master. *Be still my beating heart!*

Sir walked back out of the kitchen holding two martini glasses. When he saw her, he stopped and chuckled. "Of course you would choose that chair."

Brie didn't understand and started to get up.

"No, stay where you are. It's actually perfect." He walked over and handed her a glass. Then he looked out over the cityscape and smiled as he took a drink. Brie regained her composure, and tasted it. The martini Sir had made was slightly dirty, with just the right amount of olive brine mixed with the smooth, high-end vodka.

"Lie back, Brie. I want to enjoy the beauty you bring to my place."

She happily obliged, lying against the back of the sexy chaise, being careful not to spill. Brie lifted one arm over her head casually, knowing it would display her breasts in a pleasing manner for her Master.

"Lovely." He took another sip of his drink with a playful smirk on his lips. Brie wondered what he was thinking but she quietly followed suit, unable to stop the tremor in her hands as she brought the glass to her lips.

"We have much to discuss, you and I. However, I wish to leave the majority of it for another day. I will be putting my consultant work on hold for a few days off so we can grow accustomed to our new relationship, but in truth...I plan to play with you hard and often. Expect little rest."

Brie loved the idea of that, but her practical side took over. "Sir, I am scheduled to work tomorrow night."

He laughed out loud. "I am confident my uncle does not expect to see you so soon after your collaring."

His uncle. It sounded adorable to hear Sir call Mr. Reynolds 'uncle'. "May I call and tell him I won't be there, Sir?"

"No, that won't be necessary. I will talk to him my-self about the matter. But you will be handing in your two weeks' notice when you return to work on Monday."

Brie couldn't hide her surprise. She'd naturally assumed she would continue working with his uncle at the tobacco shop. "Yes, Master. May I ask what I will be doing instead?"

"You will begin editing your documentary. When you present it to Holloway, the film needs to be perfect. That will take time, and you won't have the time if you are stocking cigarettes on shelves."

Everything in her life had changed in one night. It was thrilling, but also a little disconcerting. "I'm grateful I can say goodbye to Mr. Reynolds and help train my replacement."

"No doubt Unc is going to have trouble replacing you."

She wanted to giggle when he called Mr. Reynolds 'Unc'. It was a casual side of Sir she'd never suspected existed, which made her more impatient to discover Sir's many secrets.

He continued on without interruption. "However, it is not my concern—or yours," he added for emphasis.

Pleasing Sir and making the documentary is my new reality? Pinch me now! "I understand, Sir... Master..." She blushed. "What should I call you?" Brie felt foolish for not knowing the protocol with him now that he was no longer her trainer.

He laughed. "It's simple, Miss Bennett. When we have a conversation or are out in public, I expect to be called Sir. However, when we are in a scene I am your Master."

She looked up at him shyly, the word 'Master' having

a distinct effect on her. "Thank you for the clarification, Sir." She took another sip of the martini to hide her nervousness.

"I shall also call you by a different name."

That was unexpected news. Brie rested the drink on her lap as she gave Sir her undivided attention. "What name is that, Sir?"

"Téa."

Brie tilted her head, uncertain of its meaning. She dutifully answered, "Thank you, Sir."

He graced her with a heart-melting smile before taking a drink.

Tay-ah... She'd never heard a sub called that at the Center. Names were significant—they helped define the role of the submissive—so she waited patiently for Sir to explain.

He set his glass on an end table and approached her with a tender look in his eye. He grazed her cheek with the back of his hand. "My father was half Italian; 'téa' means 'goddess'."

His answer left her speechless. In one fell swoop, he had graced her with a huge compliment and revealed the fact that his father was of Italian descent, but no longer living. Brie was unsure how to respond and whispered, "I am honored, Sir."

"Know that I will think of you as a goddess even as I fuck you like a slut."

His words were powerful and unsettling. Brie quivered in the red lounger and closed her eyes, trying to calm her pounding heartbeat. Was she woman enough for such a man?

"Téa, the only item you are allowed to wear is the collar around your neck."

The tingling fire began in her loins as Brie opened her eyes and nodded. She carefully set down her drink and complied with his instructions. Once she was naked, she bowed low at his feet.

"Walk to the window."

Brie rocked off her heels and stood up, floating on clouds as she made her way to the expansive window. She felt the weight of Sir's stare on her and trembled at the intensity of it. There was an acute sense of vulnerability in being naked in front of the huge window, especially with a similar high-rise just to the right of the building.

In a deep voice he commanded, "Spread your legs shoulder-width apart, put your hands on the window and lean forward so that your nipples touch the glass."

She opened her legs and put her palms on the cold window, leaning slowly forward until her nipples made contact with the chilly glass. Brie gasped softly and waited for his next instruction, but he gave none. She watched Sir's reflection in the window as he stood and admired her while sipping his martini.

The wait, the anticipation, combined with his lustful scrutiny, made Brie exceedingly wet. She closed her eyes, chagrined when she felt a trickle of her excitement run down her leg. Brie was desperate for him, her nipples aching with need, stimulated by the pressure and temperature of the glass.

Her heart skipped a beat when she heard Sir walk out of the room and the distinct sound of the martini glasses being placed on a granite counter. *It begins…*

"Don't move or speak, but you are allowed to come," he murmured as he drew close.

Brie bit her lip when Sir lightly traced her shoulder with his fingertips, her whole body concentrating solely on his touch. She continued to sneak peeks at his reflection, enjoying the erotic contrast of her being completely nude while he remained in his tux, minus the jacket.

Sir's hand trailed down her back and over the swell of her ass. Brie had to consciously stifle her cry when his demanding fingers pressed into her sex and he felt the extent of her need.

His grunt was low and passionate. "Your body betrays you. You stand quiet and demure, but inside you are a raging firestorm of desire."

She struggled to keep quiet when he began playing with her pussy, already oversensitive from need of him. With his expert fingers, he quickly brought her to a swift orgasm.

"So soon?" Sir chuckled lightly in her ear. Then he knelt down on the floor.

Brie about died when she felt his tongue on her still throbbing clit. She made a muffled squeak and closed her eyes tightly, trying to remain upright as he spread her outer lips with his fingers and took a long, drawn-out lick.

"I love the taste of Brie."

He's making a joke? She almost burst out in giggles but bit down on her lip hard enough to bring tears to her eyes.

Brie's legs trembled as Sir swirled his tongue over her clit, between her dripping inner lips, until he reached that sensitive area between her opening and her sphincter. Her inner muscles contracted powerfully. To have Sir concentrate his oral attention so close to her ass felt enticingly forbidden. Unfortunately, the area was so sensitive that her knees buckled.

Sir seemed to have anticipated it, because his hands cradled her buttocks as he gave Brie the support she needed to regain her stance. "No moving," he admonished as she returned to the same spot. Brie gasped when he pressed his fingers onto her clit and rubbed in circles slowly, causing a delicious burn.

She was completely held under his spell, his willing and wanton plaything.

"Come," he whispered hoarsely from between her legs.

Her body tensed, initially resisting the command. Soon, however, a cold chill settled on Brie, traveling through her body just before she exploded in a second release, far more powerful than the first. He licked her clit as it pulsed against his tongue.

With a will of iron, she stayed in place and only made small, whimpering gasps. As the last contraction reverberated through her small frame, Sir growled lustfully, "Your ass calls to me."

A cry caught in her throat as he coated his thumb with her juices and slipped it into her tight hole. He played with her ass while he continued to sensually torture her with his tongue. Sir began sucking on her clit in a rhythmic manner, causing her pussy to burn with unbearable heat. When he started thrusting his thumb to match that rhythm, her pussy exploded in violent pleasure.

Brie's legs shook uncontrollably as the third orgasm rolled over her. She was going to fall—there was no way to prevent it. "Sir…" she whimpered just before her legs gave out.

He chuckled as he caught her. "Can't handle your new Master?"

She looked up at him in amazement. *The power of the man…*

"Tsk, tsk," he joked as he helped her up. But then he ordered, "Resume the position, téa."

She had to look down at her feet to make sure they were spread properly, because her entire body had become weak and uncooperative. Brie put her hands on the cold glass and pressed her nipples against it. *Can a woman faint from coming?* she wondered. She knew she was in for a hard fall the instant she heard him unzip his pants.

Slow breaths, Brie… She watched Sir's reflection clandestinely as he positioned himself behind her. His hard cock pressed against her wet, overly excited pussy just before he thrust his full length into her, causing her nipples to rub against the cold glass.

Oh, dear God!

He grabbed her buttocks and thrust, each stroke pronounced and effective. Brie had to brace her hands against the glass to meet his fervent strokes. He made sure her nipples took the onslaught, and they rubbed up and down the chilly glass with each motion. Electrical jolts from the friction coursed straight to her groin.

She looked at Sir in the reflection, watching the concentration on his face as he delivered exactly what he wanted her to receive. Then he leaned into her, putting his hands on top of hers. She stared at their intertwined fingers, overcome by the sensuality of it.

Sir pressed her body against the glass, growling in her ear, "I've wanted to fuck you like this since the first day I saw you."

Brie closed her eyes and whimpered when his lips came down on her neck and he bit her as if he were a lion subduing its mate. She gave in entirely when her body embraced the chilly wave of her fourth orgasm, no longer needing to concern herself with standing. Sir held her in place with the pressure of his body against hers, his teeth still positioned on her neck. She shuddered afterwards, slowly becoming aware that her cheeks were wet with tears.

"Mine," he stated as he pulled away from her, denying himself his own release.

Brie gasped breathlessly as she realigned herself to Sir's specifications. Legs apart, hands on the glass, nipples touching it… She quivered all over, a bundle of spent energy. He knew how to dominate her mind, body and spirit. Even her orgasms, which she'd considered hers alone to control. It was a profound lesson indeed.

Lesson Two: The Heart

S ir directed Brie to the bathroom down the hall.
"Come back to me when you are refreshed, téa."

She smiled at him, loving the name he had given her.
Brie made her way to the bathroom on noodle legs,
shutting the door and leaning against the counter for
support. The beautiful collar around her neck caught her
eye when she looked into the mirror. Brie brushed it
lightly with her fingers. She then looked down at the
word he had written across her chest: 'Mine'.

I'm Sir's.

The thought of that sent a warm shiver through her.
Brie quickly cleaned herself off, then ran her fingers
through her hair and pinched her cheeks to pinken them
before returning to Master.

Sir was sitting on the couch, waiting for her. He
made a sweeping gesture and asked, "Where would you
feel comfortable sitting?"

He was giving her a choice, but Brie knew exactly
where she wanted to be. She knelt beside him on the
floor, the same way she had the first night they'd spent

time alone together at the Training Center. Thankfully, there was a throw beside the couch, which made the kneeling comfortable. She suspected Sir had placed it there intentionally.

Sir smiled down at her and petted her long, brown curls. "I approve of your choice," he murmured.

"I have longed to sit beside you like this again, Master."

She closed her eyes and reveled in the delightful sensations evoked by Sir's hand. Each time he brushed through her hair, a burst of electrical tingles traveled down her spine. The two sat in silence, absorbing the shock of this new dynamic together—and this new life.

Brie eventually braved the question that had been burning in the back of her mind since he'd mentioned it. "Sir, may I ask you a personal question?"

"Yes, téa."

"When you mentioned your father, you used the word 'was'."

"I did. However, it is not something I care to discuss tonight."

She looked down at the floor, regretting that she'd mentioned it.

Sir commanded, "Look at me."

Brie peeked up at Sir hesitantly.

"You are allowed to ask questions. I encourage it. But tonight I have other plans."

Her gaze traveled to his crotch and she noticed the hardness of his shaft outlined beneath the black material. When she looked into her Master's eyes, she saw lust reflected back.

Sir slowly unzipped his pants, releasing his rigid cock. He opened his legs wider and Brie obediently moved in between, taking his princely manhood in both hands. With slow, luscious licks and light nibbles, she loved his shaft before taking its fullness into her mouth.

The tang of her own juices still covered his cock, mixing with his pre-come. Brie moaned, savoring the taste of their blend. He pulled his pants down farther before he lightly fisted her hair and guided her. She purred, sucking harder as she moved her lips up and down his handsome shaft.

Making love to Sir with her mouth was intimate and powerfully bonding. She flicked her tongue against his frenulum and around the sensitive ridge of the head. He groaned and lay back farther on the couch, spreading his legs more. She relaxed her throat, preparing to take him more deeply, just as his cell phone rang.

Sir opened his eyes and sighed. "I have to take this, but do not stop." He fished the cellphone from the pocket of his open pants.

Brie did not want to distract him from the call by deep-throating him, so she concentrated on his balls and the sensitive spot just below them. She could hear Mr. Gallant's voice in her head: "*The perineum is the area between the testicles and the anus. Do not forget this area.*"

As she pleasured him, she couldn't help listening to Sir's side of the conversation. "No, I won't be able to make it tonight."

There was a deep rumble on the other end.

"I assure you that is not the case."

The phone erupted in a low roll of laughter.

Rytsar.

The deep rumbling continued on the other end, to which Sir replied, "Yes, I see no reason not to schedule a trip now." She could hear laughter on the other end. Brie attempted to hide her smile unsuccessfully.

"It appears my submissive is agreeable to the idea, as well."

Brie's heart melted at being called *his* submissive. A trip to Russia to visit the infamous Rytsar in his home-land would be an adventure, but truly, nothing could compare to now. She lavished even more attention on Sir's cock, wanting him to feel how profoundly she loved him.

"Fine. I'll work out the details later. I'm sure you'll understand why I am hanging up on you." Sir shut his phone with a snap and stuffed it back in his pocket. Brie took it to mean she could begin deep-throating him, and slid the head of his shaft to the back of her throat, relaxing her muscles so she could take him deeper.

"No, not yet," he stated. She released her hold on his cock and looked up at him from between his muscular thighs.

"Do you know what that is?" he asked, pointing to the stylish red lounger.

"An artful chair, Sir."

He raised an eyebrow suggestively, making her loins quiver. There was no doubt it was more than a simple lounge.

"It's called a Tantra chair, téa. Especially designed for the Kama Sutra. Are you familiar with the Kama Sutra?"

"I've heard of it, Sir. But no, I don't know anything about the Kama Sutra."

He lifted her chin up and leaned over to kiss her. "My naïve submissive, there is still so much you have yet to learn."

She smiled at him with love. "I'm honored to have you as teacher."

He nodded and then replied huskily, "And Master. Sit in the chair for me."

Her whole body trembled as she got up from the floor and lay down in the arc of the red chaise. Brie took a deep breath, trying to calm her racing heart as Sir shed his clothes in front of her, his belt hitting the marble floor with a satisfying clink. She marveled at Sir's masculine body. Dark hair covered his toned chest and powerful thighs, and framed Sir's handsome shaft, thick and physically pleasing. Truly the most beautiful cock she had ever seen—or felt.

Brie was surprised when he left her there, and instead walked down the hall of his apartment. She turned her head towards the window to look at the city lights. She loved the beauty of LA at night. It spoke of hope, magic and dreams coming true…

When she heard Sir, she started to turn her head but he ordered, "No, stay as you were."

Brie settled back onto the chair, biting her lip to stop the questions spurred by his command. She pretended to stare out at the city lights, but she was intently watching his reflection.

Sir looked as magnificent naked as he did dressed, and he carried himself with a confidence that made his being nude seem completely natural—preferred, actually.

She could tell he had something in his hand, but was unable to identify it. Brie watched as he approached her. She held her breath when he stood over Brie and gazed at her body. She saw Sir hold up his hand just before all the lights went out.

"Master?"

"Hush…"

She waited, listening to the sound of his breathing behind her. Sir eventually broke the silence with his low, compelling voice. "The dark allows for a more intense connection, both of us dependent on senses other than sight."

The experience reminded her of the hood that Master Anderson had used on her once. However, this was far more alluring because Sir would be equally challenged. The thought thoroughly aroused her.

Brie felt his hand begin caressing her thigh. He said nothing as he ran his fingers over her skin slowly, sensually. He explored her body, taking in every part as he found his way into every untouched crevice—between toes, behind knees, the sensitive area behind her ears, and even her unbearably ticklish armpits. Nothing escaped his scrutiny.

His warm hands glided over her ass, grasping and releasing, kneading her buttocks lustfully. "I love the flesh of a woman's ass. Pliable…sensuous…irresistible."

Brie purred softly in response.

He traced the letters he had written on her chest after the collaring as if he could see them. The individual letters tingled even after he removed his finger. Sir then placed her hand on his own chest, where she had written her word.

"Master, yes, but for this session you will call me Sir," he commanded.

She was curious what he had in mind, but answered quietly, "My pleasure, Sir."

As if he knew her thoughts, he added, "Everything I do has a purpose, a simple lesson for you to learn. What was the lesson of the window?"

She swallowed hard before replying, "Even my orgasms answer to you."

"Good." Sir found her lips with his fingers, leaned over her and kissed Brie on the lips. "Now I will teach you another."

Brie felt him cup her buttocks in his strong hands. Sir gently pushed her up the angled back of the chair as he climbed between her legs. "Tuck in your legs, téa."

As soon as she did, the smooth head of his shaft rested against her sex.

Still cradling her ass, he pressed his cock into her. Gravity helped the depth of his penetration as he lowered her down onto his shaft. "The beauty of the Tantra chair is that it allows for the perfect angle," he murmured, his cock nestling deep inside her.

"Sir…" she gasped as he began rolling his pelvis, using his hands to support her. Brie slid up and down the back of the chair effortlessly as he thrust his shaft into her, hitting the perfect spot with each stroke.

He sought out her lips again, the kisses tender. When he broke away his warm breath caressed her ear. "I shall make love to you now." His lips returned to her mouth.

Both his tongue and his cock expressed his deep passion for her.

Sir's lovemaking was an ethereal experience. Brie soaked in the emotional wave of it even as her body responded to his skill and expertise. She prayed it would never end. "I love you, Sir, with all my heart."

Instead of giving a verbal response, he surprised her by leaning over the side of the chair to pick up something from the floor. "Give me your left wrist."

Brie lifted it to him and felt Sir's hand trail up her arm to her wrist. He joined them together with a soft cord without the aid of light and announced, "We are bound together as one." His warm lips pressed against the binding before he lifted their hands over her head, holding her firm. He kissed her deeply then, thrusting with slow, fluid movements.

Brie was overcome by the profound gesture and opened herself completely to her Master, holding nothing back as he claimed her heart. He made love to her tenderly while he held her captive. It was the best of all worlds and for the first time she felt utterly...complete.

Sir growled in her ear just before his cock swelled and the powerful surges began, filling her body and soul with his masculine essence. She responded with a gentle orgasm of her own. It was like sweet ambrosia.

Sir slipped his free hand under the small of her back and pressed her to him possessively afterwards. They lay there in the dark; the only sound was their labored breathing. She matched hers to his and reveled in the added connection. Alone, bound together, skin against skin... Held in his tight embrace, Brie knew with confidence she would never love another as deeply as Sir—his claiming was complete.

Misguided Service

B rie woke up before daybreak to the sound of Sir's relaxed breathing beside her. She was tempted to pinch herself. Here she was, sleeping next to Sir, in *his* bed. Brie lay in the dark, drinking in the moment.

When he rolled over, she quietly slipped out of bed and made her way to the kitchen. She was determined to make him the best damn omelet known to man. She shivered as she tiptoed through his dark apartment, the chill of the marble freezing her toes.

When Brie reached the kitchen, she flicked on the light in the hallway and glanced over at the red lounger, a smile playing across her lips. Last night, Sir had taught her that he commanded not only her body, but also her heart. She sighed happily and scanned the panoramic view of the city. Considerably fewer lights than before twinkled below as LA prepared for the beginning of a new day. She caught a glimpse of Sir's white shirt on the floor beside the couch. Brie walked over and picked it up, crushing it to her chest to drink in his smell.

Brie purred, loving the sexy feel of his shirt wrapped

around her naked frame as she buttoned it up. The shirt hung down, barely covering her ass. Its thin material provided little protection from the cold, but the knowledge it was Sir's warmed her immensely.

She returned to the stylish kitchen to assemble the ingredients. His kitchen was clean and artfully decorated, like the rest of his house. Black granite countertops, stainless steel appliances and recessed lighting made it look like it belonged in a magazine. It was a bit intimidating, but Brie refused to be deterred.

She was delighted to see there was a whole carton of eggs. Plenty to make a mistake or two… She then searched through the fridge to gather the rest of the ingredients. Brie set them out before her and replayed the recipe in her mind, going over each step. She found an appropriate pan, bowl, and whisk, making only the tiniest of noises, being extra careful not to wake Sir. She sat down at his small, round kitchen table and waited for Master to wake up. Unfortunately, she was feeling too anxious to sit for long.

Brie decided it would be wise to do a quick run-through first. She cracked the eggs and separated them like a pro. She got the pan heating while she whipped up the egg whites. In no time, she had a fluffy, expertly cooked omelet sitting on a plate. *Wouldn't Marquis be proud?*

She felt kinda sad when she tossed it into the trash, but focused her energy on cutting up the veggies and shredding the cheese for the real omelet. As she was dicing up the ham, she heard movement behind her.

"Continue," Sir said as he settled down at the kitchen

table to watch. She noticed he wore only boxers. *Oh, my God—he looks hot.* Naked, dressed, or in boxers, it didn't matter—the man was a stunning example of masculinity.

Brie's heart began to race. It was one thing to cook without an audience, but to have Sir watch her... She took a few deep breaths before beginning. She cracked the eggs and groaned silently. *A shell!* She poured them into the sink and started again. This time she succeeded and quietly cheered. She turned on the burner and proceeded to whip and fold the egg mixture, sneaking glances at Sir while she worked. He remained stoic, but Brie swore she saw a slight smirk.

No matter. This morning she would prove to him that she could cook—omelets, at least. She poured the eggs onto the bubbling butter in the pan and turned to Sir. "What would you like in your omelet, Sir?"

"Put in whatever you assume I'd like."

She nodded. His odd answer made her feel a bit anxious over her choice, but she went ahead and sprinkled in a little chive, ham and sharp cheddar cheese. She swirled it around, noticing that the cheese was burning on the sides of the pan. *Crap, I'm supposed to wait to add cheese!*

Her nerves hit and she froze. It was ruined. She hesitated before tossing it in the trash so she could start again. Sir said nothing.

Brie began the process again. She almost burnt the butter, but saved it in the nick of time. She added the proper ingredients and mixed it up before putting it down to wait for it to set. Everything looked good; this would be a perfect omelet. She could just see the proud gleam in Sir's eyes when he tasted it.

She went to pick up the pan to swirl it, not noticing that Sir was behind her until he grabbed her wrist and turned her around. He lifted her onto the cold granite counter and began unbuttoning the shirt.

Brie glanced over at the eggs nervously. They would be ruined if she didn't get them off the stove now, but Sir was slow and deliberate as he unfastened the last button and slowly slid his shirt off her shoulders.

He kissed her on the collarbone and then slowly made a trail down between her breasts. The whole time, Brie stared anxiously at the eggs, but she quickly returned her attention to him when he looked up. Sir gave her a mischievous smile and kissed her on the lips.

When he pulled away, she couldn't hold it in any longer. "Sir, the eggs…"

He lifted her chin up and kissed her again, as if he hadn't heard. The unpleasant smell of burnt egg began to swirl around her nostrils. Her perfect omelet was ruined.

Without breaking the kiss, Sir pushed the pan off the burner and turned it off. Then he pulled away from her, wearing a serious expression. He lifted Brie off the counter, removing the shirt completely before asking her to sit.

Brie didn't know what was happening, but it was obvious she had failed somehow.

Sir sat across the table from her and stared at Brie for several moments before speaking. "Do you know what you did wrong, téa?"

She blushed and whispered, "I burnt your eggs, Sir."

"No."

Brie looked up at him, now suddenly far more alarmed. "Sir, did I pick the wrong ingredients?"

He shook his head once. "No. Apparently, you are unaware that you have made three grievous errors this morning."

Her lips trembled. *How?* What could she have done wrong when all she'd wanted to do was impress him?

"Shall I explain?" he asked.

Brie looked down at the glass tabletop to avoid his disappointed stare. "Please, Sir."

"Look at me."

She forced herself to look up and meet his solemn gaze.

"First, you left my bed without permission. A grave error on your part that shall not happen again. Second, you disobeyed a direct order."

She shook her head in disagreement. "No, Sir, I would never—"

He looked at her sternly. "Last night I told you that you were only to wear the collar."

She opened her mouth to protest but then nodded, realizing that he had. "Yes, you did, Sir." She looked down at her feet, completely mortified. "I am sorry, Sir. I deserve to be punished."

"Why did you disobey me?"

"I assumed it was a command only meant for the moment." She bit her lip to stop it from trembling. Once Brie had regained her composure, she added, "I never meant to disobey you, Sir. Please know that."

"I accept your apology. See that it does not happen again."

"Never, Sir."

"Never is a long time, my little sub. Do not be quick to use such words."

She looked at the table again, crushed to be failing so badly on her first morning with him. A glutton for punishment, she asked, "How did I fail you the third way, Sir?"

"You did not ask what I wanted for breakfast, or if I wanted breakfast at all."

Her shoulders slumped in defeat, but she quickly straightened them, not wanting to offend him further. "I was foolish not to ask, Sir."

"There is something you should know."

She looked up at him sheepishly. "What, Sir?"

"I hate eggs."

Her jaw dropped and she squeaked, "You do?" How could it be that her Master hated the only thing she knew how to cook well?

Sir crinkled his nose. "The smell makes me nauseous and now my whole apartment reeks."

She sat in stunned silence, feeling sick to her stomach.

"Do not fret, téa. I only punish willful disobedience. Today I was curious what you would do. In your eagerness to please, you forgot your training."

She closed her eyes. "Yes. You're right, Sir."

"Of course I am," he answered.

She snuck a peek and was relieved to see his expression was relaxed, not angry. When he motioned Brie to his lap, she literally jumped up and ran to him. He gathered her into his arms, and chuckled. "When Marquis told me the only things he was able to teach you to cook were an omelet and spaghetti, I had to laugh."

"Don't tell me you hate spaghetti, too?" she whimpered.

"I am not a fan of tomatoes."

"Oh…" she said dejectedly. Brie rested her chin on his strong shoulder and sighed. "You are going to starve because of my cooking."

His answer was quick. "No. Unlike you, I know how to cook."

She gasped, but noted the glint in his eye. "I'd say that is below the belt, Sir."

"It's the ugly truth."

Brie grabbed her stomach and grunted loudly. "It hurts, it hurts…"

Sir swatted her bottom. "You are fortunate I do not eat breakfast. Thankfully, that is one less meal you can ruin."

She basked in Sir's playful mood and traced his masculine jaw before kissing him. "Thank you, Sir, for hating breakfast. Is there any way I can make up for my lack of culinary talent?"

He furrowed his brow, stating, "No. There is nothing you can do to make up for your atrocious cooking skills."

She pouted prettily, smoothing out the wrinkles from his frown with her fingertips. "Are you sure?"

He snorted. "You will find your feminine charms have little effect on your Master."

Brie gave up and buried her head in his chest, mumbling, "I guess I'm hopeless."

He stroked her long hair and replied in a deceptively soothing voice, "Useless, yes, but not hopeless."

His sense of humor was brutal and she loved it. Brie was about to object, when he gave her a direct command. "Take a quick shower and ready yourself for me."

Those words were music to her ears. "My pleasure, Sir!" she replied, jumping off his lap and heading straight for the shower.

Lesson Three: A Matter of Ego

In less than a half hour Brie was washed, shaved, and primped. She opened the bathroom door and called out his name. "Sir?"

He answered with a low, sultry, "Come," from the front of the apartment. Brie glided over the smooth marble, wanting to make a favorable impression. Since she wasn't capable of cooking, she damn well would make up for it with her other skills. *Man does not live on bread alone!*

Sir was waiting for her beside the red chaise with a silver chain in his hand. She followed the trail of links down and saw that it was attached to a leg of the chair. "Kneel before me, téa."

Kneel before me, goddess...

Sir certainly had a way with words. Brie bowed before him and willingly accepted the cuff he secured around her ankle. "You will not be released until the lesson has been learned."

She looked up at him questioningly. "What lesson, Master?"

He smiled. "That is for you to figure out."

Brie had to hide her frustration. Mr. Gallant's up-front method of teaching was so much easier and involved a much smaller chance of failure.

Sir read her like a book. "You are no longer at the Training Center. Lessons will not be spoon-fed to you. Growth must be earned."

She bowed low, her head touching the floor. "I understand, Master." Then she added softly, "But I don't want to fail you."

Brie squealed when he picked her up. He held her so that she was eye to eye with him. "You cannot fail unless you are unwilling to try."

"Yes, Master."

His intense look communicated confidence in her abilities, and her fears receded. He set her back on the ground and slipped off his boxers.

Sir lay down on the lounger and motioned her to him. The clinking sound of the chain echoed through the room as she moved to straddle him. She couldn't help thinking of her Auction Day when she'd played Captain's pet. It brought a smile to her lips, but she let go of the memory. Brie looked down at her handsome Dom now, her heart bursting with pride that she was his—and his alone.

The red lounger was so narrow that both her feet touched the floor when she straddled him. It was a different position already, heightening the sense of adventure the chain already inspired.

"This first part of the lesson is easy. Make love to your Master."

Her eyes widened as she realized he was giving her free rein over his body. "Anything I want, Master?"

"Unless I tell you to stop."

Brie immediately leaned over to kiss him. All those weeks in class she had watched those lips, fantasized about them, and now they were hers for the taking. She lightly brushed her mouth against them, and was thrilled when he closed his eyes and groaned in response.

It seemed decadent to kiss him like that—like eating fine chocolate. She should show some restraint, some level of sophistication, but she could not. Brie kissed him over and over again. Sir met her enthusiasm by running his hands over her body, further igniting her hunger for him.

"I love you, Master," she declared, finally burying her face in his neck and breathing his manly scent. Sir was a combination of masculine musk with a hint of sweet like a summer's day; no artificial scents covered up his intoxicating smell. Brie took another long sniff, purring softy. However, she could not ignore the hard shaft cradled between her lower lips.

Brie rubbed herself against him, loving the feel of his stiff cock pressed against her sensitive clit. She used it, shifting her pelvis to enjoy different angles without letting the head of his cock slip inside. Sir did not object. He seemed to enjoy watching her pussy coat his manhood with her abundant excitement.

Alas, there was only so much self-teasing she could take. Brie lifted herself up and positioned his handsome cock so that it barely touched her opening. She teased herself for a little longer by not settling down onto his rigid manhood. She leaned over to kiss his lips again, savoring the agony of being so close to satisfaction, but delaying her own pleasure…and his.

Sir put his hands on her hips and squeezed her buttocks, but to her surprise he did not thrust. He continued to let her control the level of torturous penetration. His level of restraint did Brie in, and she ever so slowly, millimeter by millimeter, lowered herself onto his shaft. The unique chair gave her a level of control she hadn't experienced before.

Brie moaned loudly when her pussy hit the base of his cock. All of Sir. Inside her. While they kissed. *Pure, unadulterated heaven.*

"Damn, woman, you feel good," Sir said hoarsely.

Brie kissed him again, reveling in the fact her body was pleasing to Master. She began to move up and down his thick shaft, using the power of her legs. Sir helped guide her with added force so that each stroke was fully realized. No movement was wasted, making it incredibly intense.

She cried out as time after time his cock surged into her, filling her completely. He began thrusting faster as he threw his head back. A low groan rumbled in his chest.

Oh, God! To watch Sir come…

He suddenly stopped and held her hard against his rigid manhood. The pulses that had been building inside her could not be halted. She bit her lip, having not been given permission to orgasm. He opened his eyes and grinned as he started the thrusting motion again. It distracted her enough to stave off the climax.

She let out a small gasp, remembering his previous lesson. *Even my orgasms answer to him.* She trembled at his control.

Brie leaned over to give him another kiss, but felt her pussy contract when his tongue parted her lips. She had to pull back. Brie closed her eyes. *Do not come. Do not come.*

Sir's hands glided over her skin, caressing her stomach before moving up to her breasts. He flicked the nipples with his thumbs as he squeezed her ample breasts. "You're breathtaking, téa."

She automatically responded to his praises by kissing him again. This time he grasped the back of her neck as he parted her lips, claiming her mouth. She instinctively struggled to get out of his embrace in an effort to prevent what was about to happen.

"Relax," he whispered between kisses.

The instant she let down her defenses, her orgasm crashed over her. It was powerful, having been denied before. Her pussy continued to pulse long after her climax had ended.

Sir released her and grabbed her hips again. She followed his lead, moving slowly up and down his shaft, whimpering softly because of the sensitivity of her freshly-come pussy. He threw his head back again, closing his eyes and groaning loudly. Through gritted teeth he told her, "When I tell you to stop, don't move."

"Yes, Master," she breathed.

Brie watched Sir intently as his whole body stiffened. "Stop," he grunted as he pushed deep into her. She braced her hands against his chest and became still. He clenched his jaw, breathing heavily. Sir opened his eyes just before the spasms began. It was incredibly hot to gaze into Sir's eyes as he came deep inside her.

Afterwards, he turned her around without disengaging (a hidden benefit to the oddly shaped chair) and wrapped his arms around her—one around her waist, while his other hand rested comfortably around her neck in a possessive embrace. Brie closed her eyes and drank in his loving ownership.

They lay like that, in a state of peaceful harmony, for what seemed like hours. There was nothing but the beauty of now and Sir's embrace. He let out a long, satisfied sigh.

Her body flushed in response. Connecting like this with Sir was amazing, and it made her crave even more intimacy with him. Questions pricked her consciousness and she broke the pleasant silence by asking the one foremost in her mind. "Master, may I ask about your father now?"

She felt his whole body tense, but he answered evenly. "Yes."

"How did he die, Sir?"

He paused for a second. "My father committed suicide."

Brie felt her heart crush inward. The mood in the room had completely changed with his revelation. "I shouldn't have brought it up. I'm sorry, Sir."

"No." He sighed quietly. "It's important you know. Continue."

"Thank you, Sir." She paused before asking her next question, not wanting to upset him. "How old were you?"

"Fifteen."

Her sympathy poured out to him as she imagined what it must have been like to lose his father at such a pivotal age in his life. "What about your mother, Sir?"

His voice dropped an octave. "She is dead to me."

Brie shivered and stopped the line of questioning. She squeezed the arm he had wrapped around her middle.

Sir continued of his own volition, "My father was…extremely talented, a world class violinist." He readjusted himself, holding her tighter. He added, almost as an afterthought, "An unusually gifted musician who was idolized by his fans."

Brie imagined an Italian hunk with dark hair and dark, soulful eyes, standing on stage alone, playing for an enraptured audience. She couldn't help wondering how that had affected Sir growing up. Had he been close to his father or had the man been absent from his life? Had the constant traveling caused an estrangement between his mother and father? There were so many questions to ask, but at the moment she felt only empathy for Sir and remained silent.

His voice was distant when he spoke again. "I still find it difficult to believe he's gone. Such a force in the world. How can that disappear as if it never existed?"

Brie suddenly felt inadequate, not knowing what to say but feeling a need to break the deafening silence. "Death is cruel, Sir."

"Have you lost someone?" he asked quietly.

"Yes, my grandfather when he was eighty. Nothing

as great as your loss, Sir."

He tightened his hold on her. "Good. I would not wish that on anyone."

She decided her words would be useless, so she rested her head against his chest and surrounded him with loving thoughts instead.

He spoke a few minutes later. "Suicide is brutal."

"I can't think of anything worse," she answered softly.

"No, neither can I… That last image of him is seared in my brain and I will *never* be free of it." He snarled under his breath and abruptly lifted Brie off him. The chain rattled as he placed her feet on the floor. "Let's return to your lesson, my wayward sub."

Sir stood up and formally kissed her on the forehead, as if it were part of a ritual. He then pulled a mat out from under the Tantra chair and laid it down beside her. His voice changed, once again unruffled and commanding. "Kneel. Legs closed, hands behind your head so that your breasts are displayed."

After the command Sir walked away from her, his tight ass flexing as he moved. Despite the seriousness of his mood, she couldn't prevent herself from admiring it. The man was majestic naked.

Brie obediently lowered herself to the mat, wondering if she had been wrong to say anything. She looked out of the window at the clouds drifting in the sky and tried not to second guess herself.

When she heard the shower, she found herself imagining Sir's hands running over his muscular body as he lathered up. How she wished she could join in the fun.

Brie sighed, wanting to free Sir from the taint her questions had caused.

He returned to her, fully dressed, and picked up his house key from the counter. "I have a few errands to run, including retrieving your car and purse from the Training Center. Thankfully, Marquis thought to lock your handbag in the safe."

Brie had totally forgotten about those mundane, but exceedingly important, details. "That is kind of you, Sir."

"Kindness has nothing to do with it, téa. I have assigned you a task. Therefore, I will take care of this while you complete it."

"Yes, Sir," she answered meekly.

"Remain in this position until I get back. You are only allowed to release yourself to use the restroom. Be prepared to tell me the lesson I am teaching you with this."

Brie bowed her head in answer.

"And téa?"

She looked up timidly.

"Asking about my father was not an error on your part. If I hadn't wanted you to know, I would not have spoken of it."

She smiled up at him gratefully. "Thank you, Sir."

Sir nodded and left the apartment, shutting the door quietly behind him. Brie sighed as the electricity of his presence left with him, leaving behind an emptiness that weighed upon her.

Brie was unsure why Sir was having her practice kneeling again, but she felt certain it was not meant as a punishment. It concerned her that the purpose of the lesson eluded her, especially since Sir expected an explanation upon his return.

Worrying about it wasn't producing answers, so Brie closed her eyes and thought of her friend, Lea. Brie wondered what the bubbly jokester was doing the day after graduation. *Probably sleeping in...*

If Lea had to guess what Brie was up to, she would never believe Brie was enduring another kneeling lesson. It had been their first kneeling lesson at the Training Center that had marked the beginning of the girls' friendship. That day, Lea had cracked jokes when they'd been ordered to kneel quietly. Brie had chosen to stand up for her, despite Marquis' threat to punish Brie for Lea's transgression. All because Mary had decided to tattle.

Mary...

Brie's lips curled into a snarl. She could not believe the bitch had attempted to steal Faelan from her on the night of graduation. It was low, even by Mary's standards. But then, Mary had always gone after any Dom Brie had shown an interest in. Up until last night, Brie had been willing to forgive her, knowing that Mary was a hurting unit who desperately needed a friend. Brie had been foolish enough to believe that over the six-week course she'd been able to break through the barriers Mary had put up and develop a real friendship with the woman.

Yeah... I'm a freakin' idiot!

She'd been completely blindsided, never suspecting that Mary would betray her so brazenly. Brie would never forget the shock of seeing Faelan enter Mary's room, or the sounds of the bitch's cries of passion during their 'interview' together.

Thank God for Marquis…

Brie opened her eyes and let out the pent-up rage she'd been holding in since last night. "Fuck you to hell, Mary!"

In another apartment, she heard the muffled barking of a tiny dog. Even the dog hated Mary.

It didn't matter that things had worked out for the best. The simple fact was that Mary had deliberately stabbed Brie in the back by picking Faelan. But the bitch hadn't left it at that. No! She'd had to fuck him in the adjacent room, *knowing* Brie could hear them.

Suddenly Faelan's blue eyes loomed before her. He was no better than Mary. Brie understood that school protocol had required him to join Mary for the interview, but anything that had happened during the interview itself had been *his* choice. It sickened Brie to think that she had even considered Faelan as her potential Master. Thankfully, her eyes had been opened before she'd made her decision at the collaring ceremony.

Mary's treachery had inadvertently forced Brie to make the right choice. But as long as she lived, she would never forgive *or* forget Mary's betrayal.

Fuck the bitch and Faelan both!

Inside her head, she heard Mr. Gallant's voice reprimanding her for those ugly words. She rolled her eyes and reworded her thoughts, wanting to think and behave like a proper submissive. *I hope Mary and Faelan get exactly what they deserve, Mr. Gallant.*

Brie sighed in satisfaction afterwards. It did feel better not to cuss. "Thank you, Mr. Gallant," she said out loud, smiling at the walls. The only way she could remain a sub worthy of Sir's dominance was to consistently behave like one. It would not do to be submissive only in his presence. Perfect obedience at all times. *A true submissive obeys in mind and body, whether or not Master is present.*

She nodded once, confident in her fresh resolve. Brie ignored her hurting knees and aching back, staring out of the scenic window with a contented sigh. Cars inched along the tiny streets. People were busy navigating their lives while she knelt on the floor alone, anxiously waiting for *him*.

Brie wondered if Sir was thinking about her as he went about his business. Was he secure in the knowledge that his newly acquired sub was obeying his command? That she was kneeling beside his sexy Tantra chair, earnestly awaiting his return?

Brie glanced around the room suddenly, wondering if Sir had cameras, but she quickly dismissed the idea. Why would he? This wasn't the Training Center. Still, it helped to think that he was watching her remotely. It caused her to straighten her back more, keeping her lips supple and her body relaxed. Yes, that was how she would endure the wait—by pretending that even now Sir was secretly watching her, pleased with her level of commitment.

"I love you, Sir," she whispered.

Brie's heart skipped a beat when she finally heard the key turn in the lock hours later. *Master's back!* She was embarrassed to admit to herself that she felt just like a little puppy eager to greet its owner.

Sir entered the apartment and placed her purse on the counter before going to the kitchen with several bags in his hands. He didn't even glance her way as he walked by.

It was reminiscent of her objectification lesson and she actually felt an odd thrill. Brie waited patiently, although her stomach started growling when she heard him cutting up food in the kitchen.

Sir came out briefly and smiled. "Well done, téa." His words of praise thrilled her overly much, forcing her to show great restraint to avoid grinning like a fool. He commanded smoothly, "You may stand and sit on the chair, legs spread for my pleasure."

Brie choked on the groan that erupted from her lips when she tried to get up off the floor. The chain accentuated her lack of grace, making random clinking sounds as she struggled with her stiff limbs. Thankfully, Sir had returned to the kitchen and missed her graceless transfer from floor to chaise.

He returned soon after with a plate in his hand. Sir walked over and sat on the foot of the chair. "Before we eat, I want to hear what you've learned."

Her heart raced as she voiced her answer, terrified she might be wrong. "I learned two lessons, Sir."

"Go on," he said, sounding surprised.

Brie suddenly panicked. Was it okay to learn more than one thing per lesson? *Of course*, she chided herself. "Sir, it is important for me to think like your submissive at all times, even when you are not beside me."

Sir remained silent for a moment and then stated, "I

would have assumed you already knew that, after six weeks of training."

She looked at him self-consciously. "Sir, I *knew* it in my head, but I hadn't lived it until now."

He nodded. "Very well. What else did you learn?"

"The only thing I care about is pleasing you, to be worthy of your domination."

"Answer me this. If pleasing me was your motivation this morning, what went wrong?"

Brie thought back on it. Her mistake had been to assume he wanted what she would cook, but it was more than that. She had wanted to show off her meager cooking skills. Why? To prove that she was good enough for him.

"I wanted you to be proud of me."

"And why was that a problem?"

She looked down at the leather cuff around her ankle as she thought about it. "Because..." She stalled, and then suddenly it came to her. "In the end it had to do with stroking my own ego, not pleasing you, Sir."

"Exactly," he replied, holding up a bite-sized piece of green apple. "Open."

Brie parted her lips and took the apple in her mouth, appreciating its sweet tartness.

He spoke while she chewed. "I am confident in my choice of sub, despite the fact the decision was thrust upon me last night. To doubt yourself is to doubt my choice, and *that* I will not tolerate."

Sir had gifted her with a clear understanding. Even though she had chosen Sir at the collaring ceremony, the truth was it had been his choice to accept her as his submissive. In fact, he'd turned her down initially. She shuddered, remembering it, but the pain of that rejection was like a long-lost echo now.

The fact Sir cared enough to address her fear of inadequacy endeared him to her even more. Brie looked up at her Master, declaring with heartfelt conviction and a smidge of humor, "Sir, I will not doubt your fabulous choice of sub."

His eyes softened as a smirk played at the corner of his lips. "I believe you are in need of another lesson." Sir fed her another piece of apple and then took one for himself. "But this lesson is best done on an empty stomach." He got up and placed the dish in the kitchen before coming back to her. He undid the chain around the leg of the chair and started down the hallway.

"Come, téa."

A Little Restraint

Brie followed behind Sir, quivering in excitement. Having waited for him for hours, her body was revved up and ready for whatever he desired.

Sir led her into his bedroom, which was a stark contrast to the rest of the apartment. Whereas the color scheme of the rest of his place was dark and stylish, his bedroom was a sultry crimson with gothic accents of ironwork. It alluded to unspeakable acts of the sensual kind.

He proceeded to attach the chain to the leg of the bed. He then left her, disappearing into his closet before returning with several items in his hands. The one that grabbed Brie's attention was the spreader bar.

Sir noticed her focusing on it and grinned. "Oh, yes, you will be quite restrained for this session. Feel free to call a safeword at any point, for I will not be asking."

Brie's knees shook. There was no doubt Sir was going to push her limits with him. The thought both excited and terrified her. Such an experienced Dom would be used to compliant, fearless subs.

He knows you, Brie, she reminded herself.

Sir knelt down at her feet and caressed her ankle before he attached the first cuff. She felt the fire begin. His touch was like an electrical storm, sending jolts of sensation upward.

"Spread your legs," he said evenly.

Brie stared down at him as she moved to comply with his command. Sir wrapped his strong hand around her ankle to help her get the proper distance. She moaned softly as he buckled her into the cuff. Sir stood up with a satisfied look.

His eyes met hers and she caught her breath. The hunger she found in those eyes was overpowering. Sir laid out a large towel at the end of the bed and then picked her up. He placed her at the foot of the bed, pressing her stomach down onto the mattress. "Wrists."

Brie put her wrists behind her. He quickly and adeptly bound them with cord. Sir then took a silk scarf and tied it over her eyes. Her whole body was trembling by then. He'd effectively subdued her, leaving her defenseless to his ravenous appetite.

"You are mine."

"Yes, Master."

He moved to the side of the bed and she heard the lighting of a match. The scent of sulfur wafted through the air. Then the sound of music filled the room, intense and beautiful. She felt the bed move as Sir leaned over and whispered in her ear, "A favorite composer of mine, Giuseppe Verdi." Brie listened to the music, carried by the impassioned sound of violins. He moved to her other ear. "The opera is called *La Traviata*. A poignant tale of love and sacrifice. We must see it sometime."

Brie was instantly transported back to their last opera, the night he had played the role of Khan. There in the theater he had played out her King fantasy, with another male acting as the priest. God, how she had wanted him that night, but she had been denied the pleasure. Now here she was, bound and blindfolded, about to be fucked by Master. His choice of music added a sense of sophistication and substance to the intense scene.

Sir stood behind her. "The oil will be warm."

Brie instinctively jumped when she felt the first few warm drops fall on her skin, as he poured it over her lower back and down the crack of her ass. The oil was incredibly erotic as it rolled down and slowly trickled off her mound, one drip at a time. Then he began to rub the oil into her skin—first her back, then her buttocks, until Sir was concentrating all his attention on her tight little hole.

"Deny me nothing," he stated, slapping her ass resoundingly. Brie's surprised squeal rivaled the high notes of the woman singing in the background.

He growled hoarsely, "I will hear your passion as I use you for my pleasure, téa." He slapped her hard on the other cheek, causing another cry to escape her lips as she instinctively struggled to avoid the pain. The spreader bar kept her in place, her body helpless and open to his ravenous need.

The skin on her tender ass tingled as he changed tactics and played with her buttocks, lightly slapping and squeezing them—reacquainting her with the sensual power of his touch. She lay there, helpless and completely turned on.

Sir knew her, knew exactly how to make her body crave him.

His play stopped and then he left her again. She heard the sound of running water from the adjoining bathroom before he returned. Suddenly, Sir's hand was between her legs, confirming her state of desire. "My goddess is dripping for her Master."

"Most desperately, Master," she agreed.

Brie soon heard the distinct sound of Sir liberally applying lubricant to his cock. Sir was silent as he coated the outside of her anus with gel and then eased more inside her tight hole. He made sure her ass was thoroughly prepared for the pounding she was about to receive. He separated her buttocks with his slippery hands and she felt the warm head of his shaft slip into the valley of her ass.

Sir's cock rested against the entrance of her taut hole. He grabbed her hips and began pressing his thickness into her. Despite being willing, Brie's body resisted his manly conquest—making the encounter that much more exhilarating.

In the past, Sir's entering had been gentle but demanding. This time was different. He pressed into her with more force, slapping her ass lightly to weaken her resistance. "Give yourself to me," he demanded. She consciously relaxed her inner muscles and cried out as his generous shaft opened her up, body and soul.

Sir used her hips to give him leverage, thrusting deeper into her ass while the music swirled around them.

It was surreal, profound. When he was buried deep inside her, Sir grabbed her bound wrists and remained motionless, pressing even harder, forcing her to take all of him.

Brie's body struggled to embrace the fullness of Sir. She gasped and then moaned as he began moving, slowly stroking her tight recesses with his impressive cock. "I remember when you struggled to take me halfway."

Brie remembered their first encounter well. She'd had no idea then how forbidden their coupling had been. It hadn't been until the next day, when she had almost been kicked out of the program and Sir had been asked to resign, that she'd understood the ramifications. It still amazed Brie that Sir had been willing to risk his career to be the one to take her anal virginity.

Had he suspected what the final outcome would be? Had that been his method of marking his potential mate? The possibility of it excited her.

"I love your cock, Master."

"My cock loves your ass, téa."

She purred, but soon cried out as Sir held her down more securely and fucked her hard. In an instant there was nothing but Sir's cock powering into her ass. Master held nothing back as he dominated her with his formidable shaft.

Brie gasped, her face buried in the bedcovers as she desperately tried to hold on to reality. Her whole body began to tingle as it slowly moved to another level of awareness. When he slowed down and snaked his fingers below, rubbing her clit furiously, she could only gasp for air like a fish out of water.

"You are my instrument. Sing for me," he stated. The violins sounded in the background as Sir pushed deep into her and brought her over the edge with his skillful manipulation. Brie suddenly found her voice and screamed out in ecstasy.

Before the last contraction had ended, he was pounding into her again. Her body was no longer hers, transformed into his instrument of pleasure. She began crying in pure joy, loving his hands clasped around her bound wrists, the restriction of the spreader bar, the opera music swimming in her head and his masterful cock that demanded everything of her.

He suddenly changed angles and she tensed. The head of his shaft began hammering her in a spot that made angels sing. She lost all connection with her surroundings as she felt her spirit floating upwards; exploding in pure rapture the moment Sir released his hot seed.

Brie slowly came back down to a light caress on her cheek. She opened her eyes and gazed straight into Sir's, blinking several times. All her bindings had been removed and the music was now playing softly in the background, more like a whisper than a song. Sir was lying naked beside her.

"My pleasing little sub, how you do fly."

She smiled and closed her eyes again, needing to concentrate on his touch. His soothing voice gently brought her back down to earth.

"I love you, babygirl."

The Wolf Returns

B rie arrived at the tobacco shop early on Monday, but it seemed weird to her now and she actually blushed when she saw Mr. Reynolds. At her graduation ceremony, she'd found out he was Sir's uncle, and he'd seen her bare-chested.

Thankfully, Mr. Reynolds did not behave differently. He nodded as he priced the tins of tobacco. "Good to see you, Brie."

She walked up to him and smiled sadly, handing over her letter of resignation. "I'm sorry, Mr. Reynolds, but I am going to be moving on."

He took her letter reluctantly. "I can't say I'm surprised."

Jeff came up from the back. "What? Are you quitting, Brie?"

Brie ignored him—she had no respect for the boy. However, Mr. Reynolds responded to his inquiry. "Yes, we are losing Miss Bennett in two weeks."

"Fuck that. I quit." Jeff walked out of the front door without another word.

Mr. Reynolds shrugged. "Well, he just made my job easier."

Brie chuckled. It was true. Jeff had been a lazy employee who'd caused more problems than he was worth. "Will you get in trouble with the owner?" Brie asked, worried for her kind boss.

"I've wanted to fire the punk for a year. I can't be blamed if he quits."

"I'll be happy to train two people for you, sir."

He turned his head at the sound of the title she only meant informally. A smile suddenly spread across his face. "The two of you were certainly the talk of the evening after you left. I was told such a thing has never happened in the history of the Center. Are you still confident of your unorthodox choice?"

She grinned. "Yes, there is no doubt in my mind."

"Good. Thane is a good man," Mr. Reynolds said, sounding pleased. "You have balls of steel, young lady. My heart dropped when he said no."

Brie shuddered. "That was the hardest thing I've ever done, but there was no other choice for me."

Mr. Reynolds' expression changed, and she noted sadness in his eyes. "Thane has had a difficult time opening up to people ever since..."

He stopped, so she finished his sentence. "Since his father's suicide?"

Mr. Reynolds' face became pale. "My brother-in-law's death changed the boy, but walking in on it would change any man."

Brie was shocked by the revelation. Sir hadn't just seen his father's body; he had been present when the man had died. It broke her heart.

She saw the raw grief in Mr. Reynolds' eyes when he spoke. "The boy lost himself when Alonzo died. We took him in, but he was in too much pain and far too independent to accept our help. He petitioned for emancipation at age sixteen, and was granted it. I've tried to be there for him as much as he would allow." Mr. Reynolds' expression changed, as if he regretted what he'd said. "I'm sorry. It isn't my place to talk about this. Forgive me."

"It's obvious everyone was hurt by it," Brie offered. She found it odd that Mr. Reynolds hadn't mentioned his own sister. What part, if any, had she played in what had happened?

His voice caught, the emotion hard for him to contain. "It's a damn shame. An extraordinary talent lost and a young man scarred for life." He turned away and wiped his eyes before he looked at her again. "I can't tell you how grateful I am that you've come into his life."

She shook her head. "Oh, no, I'm the grateful one."

"It's good you feel that way, Brie. Thane is much like his father," he paused and smiled sadly, "in that he is honorable to a fault."

"Sir is an honorable man," Brie agreed, returning his smile. "I'm thrilled he has chosen me to partner with."

Mr. Reynolds wrapped one arm around her. "As much as I hate to lose you, I can't think of a better reason."

"At least I don't have to say goodbye." She gave him a tentative hug. "Now that I'm part of the family, *Unc*."

"You are not allowed to call me that at work. Nepotism and all that."

She nodded and stepped away. "I understand. I'm sorry, Mr. Reynolds. It won't happen again."

He laughed out loud. "I'm just kidding, Brie. We're surrounded by nepotism here. Truly, I have never had an employee who worked as hard, or treated me with the respect you do."

"I hope you are allowed to hire good people this time, Mr. Reynolds."

He shook his head. "I doubt it. I've been told there are several nieces and nephews looking for jobs."

"I'll do my best to train them well, then."

Mr. Reynolds chuckled. "You do that for me."

She spent a pleasant morning at the shop, ringing up customers and stocking the shelves. At noon, her phone binged with a text. She took a quick glance and saw that it was Sir. As texting was not allowed at work, she asked for permission before answering it. "I know it's against policy, Mr. Reynolds, but it's Sir. I really need to take this."

He smiled in understanding. "Yes, Brie. You have my permission to answer his texts only, just as long as customers are not present."

She beamed at him. "Thank you, Mr. Reynolds!"

Brie held her breath as she clicked on the text. The butterflies began when she read it. *Tonight we will play a game.*

It left her in a constant state of excitement for the rest of the day. What did Sir have planned for the evening? The possibilities gave her goosebumps.

When five o'clock finally rolled around, she bade Mr.

Reynolds goodbye and headed out, a bundle of sexual tension. *Going home to Master!*

As she was walking to the car, she heard her name being called. "Brie! Brie Bennett."

She turned and saw Faelan loping up to her. "What are you doing here?" she asked, stunned to see him at her place of work.

"I've been waiting to talk with you alone."

"I can't," she exclaimed, taking a few steps back. "I don't think Sir would approve."

"But this is between us—it doesn't involve him."

She did not feel comfortable and turned to leave, not wanting to have a confrontation with Faelan in the middle of the parking lot. He quickly caught up with her and took hold of her arm. "We're just going to talk. What's the harm in that?"

"I don't think we should," she insisted.

"Brie." Blue Eyes cocked his head and smiled sadly. "Don't you think I deserve an explanation?" His eyes drew her in and she became acutely aware of the pain behind them.

"Todd…" She quickly corrected herself, addressing him properly. "Mr. Wallace."

He shrugged off the formality, calling her by her given name. "Brie, we are two of a kind, you and me." When he came nearer, she decided not to bolt. *We have to talk this out sooner or later.* "I knew the minute I met you that you and I were meant to be. Hell, my one thought this whole time has been to become the man, the Dom, you needed."

She shook her head indignantly, remembering how

he'd made her feel on graduation night. "It didn't appear that way at my graduation."

"Blossom."

She stiffened when he used his pet name for her. "Don't call me that."

"Fine." He put his hands in the air as if in surrender. "But you need to know that I didn't touch Mary."

Brie turned towards her car, not wanting to hear his version of that night. "I heard her, Fae...Mr. Wallace! Don't even go there."

He advanced cautiously, as if he were afraid she might get spooked and run if he moved too fast. "Mary needed a little pain, so I delivered what she asked for. There was no sex involved."

She glared at him. "If that was the case, you should have explained it to me when I asked, but you didn't! And now it doesn't matter." She took a defiant stance with her hands on her hips and her head held high. "I'm Sir's now. There is no going back."

Pain washed over those ocean blues, but he said with conviction, "We are meant to be together, Brie." He backed her into the side of her car, putting an arm on either side of her. "Headmaster Davis stole you from me." His stare pierced her with its intensity. "Why the hell did he spend all that extra time training me just to steal you away?"

Faelan's close proximity felt as if it were a force, immobilizing her. It needed to stop—it *had* to stop. She gazed into those deep blue eyes and said softly, "I chose him."

He snarled, "It's because of that damn Mary, isn't it?

She's the one who screwed it up for us."

"No, but she helped me to realize I can't trust you." He was about to interrupt, so she forged ahead. "When I asked if you wanted Mary, you answered, 'Yes'. I knew then you didn't care about me."

"What? Did you expect me to lie? Any guy who told you he wasn't attracted to the girl would not have been telling you the truth. Come on, Brie…" He lifted her chin, forcing her to look at him. "Just because I find her attractive doesn't mean I want to collar her. I was clear about that."

His answer threw Brie off. She scooted from under his arms and walked to the driver's side of her car.

Todd stated quietly, "I deserve a chance."

She attempted to unlock the door with a trembling hand. "None of this matters. It's too late."

"I need you, blossom." He was beside her again, covering her hand with his. "You are my reason."

She slowly pulled the key back out of the lock and looked at him. "No…"

"Brie, I didn't understand who I was until I met you. You opened my eyes to the truth and freed me from the hell I've suffered. Don't turn your back on me now."

She shook her head. "Please…stop."

"If you knew the truth you would not be so callous towards me now."

"I'm not being callous, Todd. But this," she gestured at the two of them, "doesn't do either of us any good. We can't change what happened. I—"

Faelan lifted his hand to caress her cheek. She turned her head to avoid his touch just as Mr. Reynolds opened the door of the shop and called out to her. "Brie, is this man harassing you? Do you want me to call the police?"

Brie shook her head. "No, everything is fine, Mr. Reynolds. We're done here. I was just leaving." She unlocked her car door and looked back at Faelan. "Don't talk to me again. You'll only get yourself in trouble." She jumped into her car, grateful for her boss' interruption.

On the drive home, she debated whether or not she should tell Sir. She decided against it. Faelan had been hurt enough, and Brie didn't want to add to his pain by making Sir furious at him.

But how disconcerting to find out that Blue Eyes hadn't fooled around with Mary. It didn't change her heart, because she knew without a doubt she was with the right man. However, it made her sad.

She hoped Faelan would be able to move on. It would be a shame if Blue Eyes walked away from the lifestyle because of her. Sir had mentioned seeing Faelan's natural talent and she'd had the pleasure of experiencing it herself. There was no doubt he would make some submissive very, very happy.

Sir was not home when she arrived. The first thing she did was undress so that she was naked except for the beautiful collar around her neck.

While she waited for him, she decided to cut up a salad. She might not be able to cook, but she was capable of cutting vegetables. As she searched through the refrigerator she noticed a lone tomato. It melted her heart. Sir hated the little red fruit, which could only mean one thing: he'd bought it specifically for her. She picked it up and kissed it before placing it back in the fridge to admire.

Once the salad was prepared she went to the door, choosing to greet Sir in the kneeling position he had assigned her at the Center. Her stomach was full of butterflies every time she heard the elevator open. A whole day away from Sir had her anxious to please her handsome Dom.

While she waited, she reflected on Mr. Reynolds' revelation of the deep pain Sir carried. It made her love him all the more. If love could heal wounds, she would love Sir to wholeness.

Her heart sped up when she finally heard the key in the lock. She bowed her head when the door opened. She heard it shut and then felt Sir's hand on her head, along with the familiar jolt of warm passion his touch inspired.

"Stand and serve your Master, téa."

His words warmed her loins. She gracefully stood up and felt his finger under her chin. She lifted her head up and he kissed her. Brie's soul sighed in contentment. "Welcome home, Master."

"How was your day?" he asked as he placed his key on the counter and unbuttoned his jacket. She took it from him and hung it on the hook in the hallway.

"It was good, Sir. Jeff quit, which made the day so much nicer."

Sir chuckled. "I can imagine Unc was pleased by

that."

"Yes, he was, Sir. Now I can train both replacements for him. I hope to do Mr. Reynolds justice by training hard workers."

He smiled down at her. "No reason not to try, my optimistic little sub." Sir handed her his briefcase. "Set it by the couch and wait for me there."

While she followed his orders, he disappeared down the hallway. She stared out of the large window, thrilled by this new life of hers. Sir was an exceptional person, and not just an experienced Dom. He was caring and conscientious in everything he did. Truly, she was the luckiest sub in the world.

He returned wearing only black sweatpants. His toned chest begged to be caressed and kissed. Sir sat on the couch and motioned for her to lay her head on his knee. He began petting her hair as he had each night since her arrival. It was something she adored; the ritual made her feel especially cherished.

After more than a half hour in silence, he spoke. "Today was quite successful. I have procured another client. A large client, in fact. Now that I am free of the Training Center, I plan to expand my accounts overseas. Mark my words, your Master will become a prominent force in the business world, téa."

She looked up at him, beaming with pride. "I am not surprised, Sir. You are exceptionally talented. I'm positive you would succeed in anything you tried your hand at."

He caressed her cheek. "Such blind confidence, but I appreciate your certainty." His finger traced the outline of her lips. "I must admit, it seems odd not to be at the Center tonight. Normally, I would be sifting through the paperwork of the new recruits." His hand trailed down to her chest. "However, I find this far more pleasurable…"

Brie closed her eyes and purred inside as he fondled her breasts. Sir made her feel fiercely feminine and desirable. Her body responded to her Master, her loins longing for his cock, her nipples aching for his mouth's attention.

"Are you ready to play my game, téa?"

Her heart beat rapidly when she answered. "Yes, Master."

Sir's cell phone rang on the counter. Its unusual ring made Sir stir on the couch. "Lie on the Tantra chair and play with yourself while I take this."

Brie kissed his hand reverently before she got up and walked to the red chair. She lay down and closed her eyes as she ran her fingers over her ever-wettening pussy. Just knowing Sir was going to play with her had her close to coming.

Sir's smooth voice filtered through her naughty thoughts. "This is an unexpected surprise." She opened her eyes and was startled to see a serious look on his face. "I understand. No, I am grateful for the information."

He hung up and glanced over at her. "Change of plans. I'll be leaving for a bit. Have dinner waiting for me when I return. I don't care what you make."

Brie stopped rubbing her clit and sat up. "Master?"

"An unexpected complication has come up. I need

time to sort it out," Sir stated as he exited through the front door.

She was worried for Sir. He had been so elated about his new client and now he was facing a serious setback. The fact Master had asked for dinner, knowing her cooking skills, meant that he was so distraught he didn't care what he ingested.

Brie went to the kitchen and began her best attempt at baked chicken to go along with the salad she'd made. She googled how to cook breast meat so that it would not be so dry, a common problem whenever she cooked meat. While it baked, she set the table, smiling as she imagined them sitting together, eating her simple but lovingly made meal. She hoped that Sir still planned to introduce her to his game. It had been frustrating to have it end just as it was about to begin.

An hour later, Sir returned and joined her at the table. He still seemed lost in thought, but smiled when she placed the chicken in front of him. Sir asked her about her day again, as if he'd forgotten that they'd talked about it earlier.

Brie decided to entertain him with a conversation she'd had with an older customer who loved dogs—all kinds of dogs. She shared how the elderly gentleman had gotten out his wallet and shown her at least twenty different canines he'd had the privilege to own. She laughed. "It was as if he was showing me his grandchildren. It was sweet, Sir."

Brie felt a pang of guilt at not mentioning her encounter with Todd. However, she'd noticed that he hardly touched his meal and didn't want to add to his stress. Besides, there was no point in getting Faelan in trouble over nothing.

When Sir announced he was done, he ordered her to join him over at the couch once she was finished with the dishes. She glanced at him several times as she made quick work of the kitchen. Sir was entrenched in paperwork, poring over a presentation he was going to give the next day. He hardly noticed when she knelt at his feet.

Brie didn't mind. It was an honor to watch him work and she felt doubly blessed when he shared his presentation with her before bed. Sir was an inspiring speaker, leaving her in no doubt why he was highly esteemed in the business community.

When he finished, she smiled. "If they follow your suggestions, Sir, there is no reason they shouldn't see an immediate increase in production."

"That is the key," he replied. "It is one thing to be presented with what needs to be done and another thing entirely to follow through with those changes. My job is to motivate that change."

She blushed. "I guess you do the same with businesses that you do with submissives."

He did not reply as he gathered his papers and turned off his laptop. She expected to be ordered to pleasure him orally; in fact, she had been counting on it. Instead, he stated, "You have failed me tonight." With that, he got up, turned off the lights and walked to his bedroom.

Brie's heart jumped into her throat. He *knew* about Todd's visit at the tobacco shop! He'd been waiting all night for her to say something about it.

She closed her eyes, realizing that it must have been Mr. Reynolds on the phone earlier that evening. It was natural that he would want to inform his nephew about Faelan's visit. She didn't blame him. No, this was her own fault. In trying to spare everyone from unnecessary distress, she had managed to make things so much worse.

It disturbed her that Sir wasn't even asking to hear her side of the story. Brie remained on the floor, feeling like an idiot. "Sir…" she called out.

He answered by shutting the door.

Tears rolled down her cheeks. It had been a terrible mistake not to say anything. She understood that now. All she wanted was to make things right with Sir. Whatever he demanded as punishment would be fine, as long as he could forgive her for the mistake.

Brie laid her head on the couch, feeling utterly bereft. She spent the night kneeling beside the couch in the dark, watching Sir's bedroom door. She noted when the light finally went out and stared at the door all night long, praying the light would turn back on and he would come for her.

Sir did not.

Repentance

Brie was on alert when she heard him stir in the morning. She heard the shower and a short time later his bedroom door opened. She waited with bated breath as he walked down the hallway to her. Sir was fully dressed in a business suit, his hair still slightly damp.

He did not waste time, coming directly to her and commanding, "Stand."

With great difficulty, Brie urged her stiff limbs to support her wobbly legs. She dared not look him in the eye.

"Not speaking of the encounter with Wallace is the same as lying."

"I'm sorry, Sir. I did not mean to lie to you."

"What possible reason would make you keep it from your Master? Do you respect me so little?"

She braved a look at him, wanting Sir to know her heart. "No, Master! I didn't think it was important enough."

"Anytime another Dom touches my sub, it is very much my business."

She bowed her head. "I didn't think of it that way, Master."

"Do you have feelings for the boy? Is that why you covered it up?"

"No, Sir. I love you. I want no one else."

His voice became deadly serious. "Know this, Brie." For the first time, her name sounded distasteful on his lips. "I consider you talking to another Dom without my permission an act of betrayal on your part."

The air left her lungs.

"I will not abide disloyalty."

She could barely get the words out. "I understand, Master. I deeply regret my actions."

"Any interaction with a Dom is worthy of my attention. A lie of omission is still a lie."

She bowed on the ground before him. "I understand, Master. I will not lie to you again."

"No, you will not. Look at me." Brie looked up at his imposing stature, afraid and in awe of him. "I must know the real motivation behind your deception."

She swallowed once, to force her throat to relax enough that she could speak. "I did not want Mr. Wallace to get in trouble, Master. I felt guilty that I caused him pain by choosing you, and I didn't want to add to it by making you angry with him."

"Foolish," he growled. "Wallace is a grown man. He knows the protocol. If he chooses to ignore it, he *must* suffer the consequences."

Her heart sank for Faelan. Instead of sparing Todd, she was certain she had made things much worse for him. "I understand, Master. I was wrong and deserve to be punished."

"Yes, your willful disobedience must be addressed."

As much as she hated being disciplined by Sir, she craved it, because it would put her right with him. Harmony with Master was all she wanted, and she would do anything to get it back.

"Get ready for work. You will spend the day out of contact with me. When you return home, I want you to remain fully dressed while you wait. I will dole out your correction tonight."

Sir grabbed his key and left the apartment. Brie slowly pulled herself up off the floor and headed to the bathroom. Her sense of failure was so great, she could taste it in her mouth.

The day was a trial. Mr. Reynolds knew there was something wrong, but wisely chose not to get involved. Instead, he interviewed the owner's family members applying for the job. Since there were four of them, it gave her boss some control over who would be working with him. Brie took care of the front, and spent the rest of the time taking inventory to keep her mind off her troubles.

It made for a long and terrible day. She dreaded going home to Sir, but longed to be in his good graces again. This would be her first punishment by her Master. Would he be like Ms. Clark, and use an instrument to bring pain? The thought frightened her, but she would willingly submit to his authority and endure it.

When she arrived home, she had to wait in the oppressive silence of the apartment. It was actually humiliating not to undress, because it only highlighted the fact she was not pleasing to Sir. She knelt by the door and listened to the lonely ticking of the clock in the kitchen. Each tick accentuated the dread building in her heart.

He came home just as the sun disappeared behind the horizon. The apartment was dark when Sir opened the door. He flicked on the light and walked past Brie, setting his key on the counter. She heard his retreating footsteps as he walked to his room.

Several minutes later, Sir returned and addressed her. His voice was detached and unemotional. "I will not touch you until your punishment is complete."

Not to have his reassuring touch made this horrible moment that much harder, and a tear fell down her cheek.

"Why are you being corrected?"

"I failed to tell you of my interaction with Mr. Wallace, Master."

"Why is that unacceptable?"

"No Dom is allowed to interact with me without your consent. My silence is the same as lying, Master."

"Are you repentant?"

"Yes, Master." A sob escaped her lips. "I am deeply sorry."

"Then I shall correct your repentant heart," he replied. Sir proceeded to place a ball gag in her mouth and secured it tightly around her head, being careful not to touch her with his hands. "The gag represents your willful silence."

Her jaw stretched uncomfortably to accommodate the gag, and then the saliva began to build. She understood it was an appropriate instrument of punishment for her transgression.

"You acted like a disobedient child, therefore I shall treat you like one. Go to the kitchen and get the bag of rice."

She quickly retrieved the rice and handed it over to him with her head bowed. She couldn't imagine what he had in mind.

Sir took a handful of rice and spread it in a line on the floor. Then he took a second handful and covered the line with another layer. He handed the bag back to her. "Put it away and return to me."

She did so with trepidation. What did the rice represent?

"Because you are unworthy to be naked before me, pull your pants up so that your knees are exposed." She did so, watching with mortification as a long strand of saliva escaped her mouth and dribbled slowly to the floor when she bent over to roll up her jeans.

"I do not enjoy punishing you."

She actually felt bad that her actions were forcing Sir to do this, and bowed her head lower in shame.

"Kneel on the rice with your weight resting on your knees."

Brie knelt down slowly, positioning both knees on the hard little pellets. It didn't become painful until she did as he commanded and put her full weight on her knees. She moaned in distress, the ball gag muffling her cry of discomfort.

"You will remain this way for twenty minutes."

He went to the couch and began his work. She

watched from the floor, trying to ignore the agony each tiny grain caused as it dug mercilessly into her knees. It seemed unreal that something so miniscule could cause such considerable pain.

As the clock ticked away the minutes, she tried to blink away the tears. Although it hurt, it was knowing she'd disappointed Sir that made the punishment truly unbearable. Thinking on it, she realized that not mentioning her encounter with Faelan was the same as putting the boy before Sir. It was glaringly clear to her now.

Being completely open and honest with Master was the only thing that mattered. How it affected others was not her concern. Brie accepted the pain as her obligation as a disobedient submissive. She would learn from it and would not let it happen again.

When the twenty minutes were up, Sir spoke to her again. "Get the broom and dustpan. Clean up your mess and then come stand before me."

Brie could not immediately stand because of the debilitating pain, and was forced to roll to one side. She brushed off the rice still clinging to her skin and pulled her knees to her chest, wrapping her arms around them, rocking gently to comfort herself. Once the torturous ache had subsided enough for her to stand, she picked herself up and did his bidding before presenting herself before Master.

Sir put his work down and stood up, holding a small towel in his hand. He undid the ball gag, and cleaned up the copious amounts of spittle that came with it. Once she was presentable again, he spoke.

"Have you learned your lesson?"

"Yes, Master. I will not keep anything from you in the future."

"Fine. You may undress, then."

With stiff movements, she took off her clothes and laid them in a neat pile beside her.

Sir held out his hands to her. "It's okay, téa. I forgive you."

Brie broke out in a sob and fell into his arms. He picked her up and carried her to his bedroom, then laid her down on the bed. After he'd shed his clothes Sir joined her, gathering her into his protective embrace. She could not stop the tears as she cried against his chest. Sir allowed her to weep, holding her tight. Eventually he whispered, "Hush now, Brie. You are my good girl."

There was no hot sex afterwards, no sexual games, just a Master holding his repentant submissive in the dark.

"I love you, Sir." Being reconnected with him was like being given a new lease on life. She felt she would burst with joy.

Sir nuzzled her neck and then bit down hard. She instantly became putty. "Tomorrow we are going to visit the Training Center."

"Why, Sir?" She gasped as he began sucking on the delicate skin of her throat.

"There is something I want to show you." Brie whimpered in pleasure, a host of images filling her mind. "Oh yes, my little sub. It's about to get rough for you…"

Visiting the Center

B rie stared at Sir as the first of the sun's rays flooded through the window. His face took on an almost boyish quality while he slept. It was sexy and so incredibly sweet. She was tempted to gently caress his cheek, but Sir must have sensed her inclination because he opened his eyes.

Brie gasped softly, her whole body quivering.

"Morning, téa."

She broke out into a shy smile. "Good morning, Master."

"Waking up to your beautiful face has moved me." He threw back the covers so she could admire his hard awakening. "Service me."

Her smile grew wider as she crawled between Sir's legs and took him into her mouth. Brie lavished her love with an eager tongue, swirling around his smooth head before sucking lightly to bring added pleasure. She moaned when he fisted her long hair and began guiding her with his hand. Did Sir know it melted her insides when he did that?

"I love starting the morning with your pink lips wrapped around my cock."

She looked up at Sir as she continued to suck his handsome manhood. He pushed her down deeper on his shaft and she gladly took its fullness, letting the head of his cock slip down her throat.

"Oh yes," he growled.

Her muffled moan expressed the pleasure she felt from being his. Sir was not rough, but always demanding. He had a way of using her for his own gratification, but making her feel completely cherished in the process.

Brie's pussy pulsed of its own accord in response to his pleasure. When he released deep in her throat there was a significant exchange of power: his male dominance over her, and her total submission to him—balance. It was the perfect way to start the day.

Afterwards, Brie laid her head on his thigh and looked up at him lovingly. Sir stroked her hair with a contented look on his face. "Tonight we shall visit the Center. I hope you are ready for what I have planned."

Her loins contracted with a mixture of excitement and trepidation.

Brie spent the day at the tobacco shop showing the two newest employees the ropes. It looked like Mr. Reynolds had at least *one* good worker. The niece was a whiny little thing, complaining constantly and texting her friends instead of listening. Brie knew Laurel would be nothing but a pain for her soon-to-be ex-boss, a perfect replacement for Jeff. However, the nephew was acceptable. Mike was a quick study and showed respect towards Mr. Reynolds. Brie was tempted to tell Mr. Reynolds to fire the girl and only keep the boy, but her boss had no real control over the hiring at the shop.

When she arrived home, she was surprised to find that her entire apartment had been moved into the spare bedroom and the large room was now completely stacked with boxes and cheap furniture. Upon entering Sir's bedroom, she noticed her old uniform laid out on the bed. It was exactly the same: the dark brown mini-skirt and leather corset, as well as the six-inch heels. However, the crotchless pantyhose had been replaced with lace garters and silk thigh-highs. The thong was noticeably missing.

She picked up the card that was lying on the bed and read his note:

> Had your belongings moved. We will discuss
> placement later.
>
> Dress in your uniform and wait for me at the door.

Brie dutifully dressed, feeling nostalgic as she tightened the laces of the corset and slipped on the fuck-me heels. She took a quick peek at herself in the mirror before leaving the bedroom, looking herself over critically.

Would people confuse her for a trainee at the Center because of the outfit? She turned her head from side to side and twirled slowly, staring at her reflection. The garters and new hose were a sexy touch, giving her a more refined look. The collar certainly helped state her position, but she still felt very much like a trainee in the outfit. Was that Sir's point?

She settled down before the door and waited for her Master to come. Exactly at six, she heard the key in the lock. He walked in and graced her with a pleased smile. "Ah, my little student. Are you ready for class to begin?" He placed a hand on her head and commanded, "Stand and serve your Master."

She stood before him as he held out his arm. She was mortified when her stomach growled as she was wrapping her arm around his. He looked down at her and smiled knowingly.

Brie felt the heat rise to her face. How unsexy to greet Sir with a growling stomach.

He made no mention of it, but when Sir got to the car he reached behind his seat and pulled an apple out of his briefcase. "I believe in the adage, 'An apple a day…'"

Brie took the apple and murmured, "Thank you, Sir." She smiled to herself as she bit into the tart apple, grateful she had such a thoughtful Master.

He remained silent on the drive, leaving Brie free to conjure up all kinds of different scenarios Sir might try on her. He had specifically mentioned the night before that things were going to get rough. What did that mean? Was he going to test her pain tolerance? The thought of that was definitely *not* sexy, but she trusted him to bring her through it if that was his intent.

Perhaps he was going to punish her further for her deceit involving Faelan? Brie quickly dismissed that idea.

She knew in her heart that Sir was a fair man. She had endured the punishment for her indiscretion and had received his complete forgiveness.

Brie licked the sweetness from her lips as they pulled into the Training Center parking lot. It was strange to be back, knowing she was no longer a student.

Although classes for the Submissive Training Center were on hiatus, the business college was still in full swing and the parking lot was full. Unlike before, Sir did not park in the spot reserved for the headmaster of the Center. It remained empty, announcing the fact that a new one had not been appointed yet. It gave her a pang of guilt knowing Sir had stepped down from his position to become her Master. She wondered if he was feeling similar pains of regret.

"I will open the door for you, téa," he stated. The use of her sub name let her know the protocol. She was to treat him as Master at the Center. No eye contact with other dominants and no speaking unless spoken to by her Master.

As he helped her out of the car, he ran his hand down the length of her curves. Goosebumps followed. Such simple contact, but it instantly set her focus on him and reminded her of the power of his caress.

They walked into the school, arm in arm. The receptionist greeted him. "Good evening, Headm—I mean, Sir Davis. It is good to see you again."

"Likewise, Miss Lewis."

He continued to the elevator, putting his arm around Brie when a group of students walked past. Brie kept her eyes lowered, basking in his manly protection.

Sir took her down a wing of the school she had never been before. As she passed through the doorway, she read the word *Faculty Lounge* on the gold plate. The scent of rich tobacco filled the air along with the sound of many familiar voices.

"Couldn't stay away, I see," Master Anderson said. He came over to Sir and slapped him on the back with the same casual familiarity the two had shared the first time she'd been introduced to him.

"I have no problem staying away, but damn if you people didn't insist I come back."

Master Coen's voice rang out from the other side of the room. "I apologize, but we didn't anticipate assigning a new headmaster just before a new session. There are many loose ends to be addressed."

"So you say," Sir answered jokingly. "I accept it as the price I must pay to have free rein of the place after we are done here today."

Brie's insides quivered at the thought of Sir unleashed.

A woman's soft voice floated through the air. "How are you, Sir Davis? Are you happy with your new submissive?" Brie kept her eyes glued to the floor. Her mind raced to place the feminine voice, quickly identifying her as the Asian Domme who owned Boa. Boa, the sub with a python for a cock.

Brie held her breath, waiting for Sir's answer. Would he expose her mistake with Faelan in front of the other trainers?

"I'm finding the experience challenging and *quite* stimulating."

Master Anderson laughed. "I bet you are, Thane. You picked a fine one to partner with. She won't let you rest, I wager." He hit Sir so hard on the shoulder that he momentarily lost his balance. "I have to admit though, I was a little put out when you stepped down. It was enjoyable working with you, reminded me of our college days."

Sir's low chuckle was like music to Brie's ears. "College was—"

Master Coen interrupted their reverie. "Enough of the reminiscing, we have work to do. Where's Clark?"

The door opened as if on cue and Ms. Clark's voice rang out loud and clear. "Back already, Davis? Wait... Miss Bennett, what are you doing here?" The woman stopped abruptly in her tracks and said sarcastically, "You do realize this is a *faculty* lounge."

Sir's reply was controlled, but with a slight edge to it. "Address me, Samantha. Not my submissive."

Oh, what fun having Sir correct Ms. Clark on her behalf! Brie wished she could peek just to see the look on the female trainer's face.

"Forgive me, Sir Davis. I am still wrapping my head around the fact you broke all protocol and collared a student. My apologies."

"It is precisely due to protocol that I resigned, Samantha," he said dryly.

Brie heard the disdain in his voice when he used Ms. Clark's given name. But *why* was he calling her by her first name? Did they have a history together?

"It was foolish," Ms. Clark snorted. "We've lost a perfectly good headmaster and the Center's reputation has been compromised because of your impulsive actions."

Mr. Gallant's warm voice filled the room, making Brie's soul sigh in happiness. "That is not true. Although people are certainly talking about the Collaring Ceremony, I have not heard any ridicule towards the school, nor towards Sir Davis himself. Do not exaggerate, Ms. Clark."

There was one voice that was suspiciously silent. *Marquis Gray.*

"Regardless of your opinion, Samantha, I am asking that you treat Miss Bennett and I as you would any D/s couple. You are not allowed to speak to her directly without my permission."

"Fine," she snapped. "But I demand your submissive leave the faculty lounge."

"Fair enough," Sir responded. Before commanding Brie to leave, he addressed Master Coen. "I did have a question for you."

"Certainly," Master Coen replied, moving across the room to join him.

"Would you be able to fashion an iron brand for me?"

"Not a problem. What is it you want?"

"The letter 'T', exactly an inch in height and half an inch wide.'"

Brie gasped. *A brand?*

"That should be easy enough. How soon do you need it?"

Sir's voice was pleasant when he answered. "There's no rush."

"Good, then I'll start work on it after we get the new recruits settled in."

"That should be fine." Sir turned to Brie and said, "Téa, Ms. Clark is correct. Submissives normally stay in another room at the end of the hall to your left. I will collect you after our work here is concluded."

She stole a glance at him when she answered, hoping to gain some insight into the exchange he'd just had with Master Coen. "Yes, Master."

The mischievous twinkle in his eyes let her know he had plans for that brand—and they most definitely included her. A chill coursed down her spine. Did he mean it as a warning or an honor?

Brie bowed to Sir before quietly leaving the room. She let out a huge sigh once the door was closed. She was concerned about Marquis' absence, but it was the brand that had all of her attention. She had not forgotten the day Master Coen had convinced her he was going to brand her with the school logo. She shuddered, feeling quite certain that Sir was not into 'mind fucks' the way Master Coen was.

No, Sir had already warned her that everything he did had purpose. She didn't believe for one second it was meant as a joke. There was a lesson there she was expected to learn. She shook off her trepidation as she pushed open the door to the new room.

To her surprise, Boa was sitting on a couch. He nodded at her. "Ah, it's Brie. The sub who captured the headmaster. You have quite the reputation around the Center these days."

"Good or bad?" she asked, sitting down on a lounge

chair opposite him. The smell of food caused her to sneak a quick glance at the table laden with gourmet fare. It reminded her of her training nights. She was curious why so much food had been laid out when there were only two of them.

"It all depends on who you ask. Subs who were hoping to snag the headmaster themselves are quite pissed at you, but the rest of us are rather impressed. You've done the impossible." He clapped his hands lightly in mock appreciation.

"You should know that I was never so terrified in my life."

"Ah, but for good reason. You dared to offer yourself in the face of certain failure."

Brie didn't care to relive that moment and was relieved when her stomach growled loudly. "Do you mind if I get myself something to eat?"

"Not at all."

She got up and tried to be lady-like as she filled her plate with smaller portions than her hunger demanded. It was weird to be in the same room with Boa. They'd done a scene together—a very hot scene—and here they were, just talking like casual acquaintances.

Brie dropped her napkin and bent down to pick it up, completely forgetting her lack of panties.

"Damn..." Boa replied.

She quickly stood up and grabbed another napkin. She walked back to the seat feeling the heat of her blush when she noticed his large cock straining against the tight confines of his jeans.

"My Mistress will not be pleased if I have a hard-on

when she comes to retrieve me."

"Sorry," she mumbled, taking a huge forkful of salad and looking towards the door.

"You can bet my Mistress is chuckling to herself right now, fully expecting to catch me with a stiffy so she can punish her randy sub. But I won't let that happen." He readjusted himself, pushing down on his massive cock as if it were a mischievous animal. "Tell me about your childhood," he blurted. "Make it something sad."

"Oh, um… sad, you say?" Brie's childhood had been fairly easy: good parents, stable family life, and excellent care because she was an only child. Although her parents had never had extra money, all of her needs were met. There was nothing notable about her childhood other than that horrible experience at school. "Well, I suppose I could tell you something I've shared with my trainers at the Center. When I was twelve, my family moved to a predominantly black neighborhood. I didn't have any siblings, so I pretty much had to fend for myself.

"Most of the families were struggling to make ends meet, just like us. Looking back on it, I guess I became the token punching bag to release their frustrations on. The ring leader was Darius. I don't know why he had it out for me, but just seeing my face upset him. He'd have his friends wait until I was off school grounds before they pounced. I told my teachers, but they just shrugged it off saying it wasn't their problem because it wasn't on school property."

Brie growled under her breath. "He never played fair. There were always three or more. He'd hold me down while the girls kicked me in the gut." She closed her eyes, lost in the feelings of helplessness it conjured up. "I didn't tell my parents. My dad finally had a job and there was no way I was going to ruin it for him." Brie opened her eyes, smiling sadly. "Darius was smart. The attacks always happened off school grounds and they never hit me in the face. I was able to hide the bruises."

Boa looked down at his crotch. "It's helping, please continue."

Brie rolled her eyes, amazed that her life story was being used as an erection detractor. "Everything changed the day he used the needle..." Her breath came faster as she relived that day again. "He had me on the ground, pushing my face into the dirt and telling me to eat it. I refused. He spat in my face and ordered the others to hold me down. He looked around wildly until he spied a used needle lying by the fence. When I saw him going for it, I started to kick and scream. He picked it up and ordered them to turn me over onto my stomach. I was screaming bloody murder by the time he got close to me, so Darius ripped off my shoe and stuffed one of my socks in my mouth. 'If you won't eat the dirt then you must pay the price,' he declared before he started stabbing me in the ass with the needle."

Brie closed her eyes and forced herself to calm down before she continued. "The others suddenly got quiet and let me go—like they knew a line had been crossed. I guess I must have totally freaked out because I remember screaming hysterically and then the next thing I knew, I was standing in the principal's office."

She snorted in disgust. "You know what's funny? At first, I wasn't taken seriously. I was forced to pull down my panties in front of both the principal and vice principal to show them my wounds before they believed me. My parents were called and I was rushed to the emergency room for tests."

Boa was now leaning forward, engrossed in her tale.

"I was too young to be worried about AIDS or all the other countless things the needle could have carried. No, you know what I was terrified of?"

He shook his head.

"My parents." She smiled sadly. "It went down just as I feared. My dad quit his job. Mom and I lived in a shelter for over half a year while my dad searched for another one. He eventually found work in Nebraska and that's where I stayed until I moved out here."

Boa's cock was completely flaccid by the time she finished—her work complete.

He tilted his head charmingly and surprised her by saying, "Everyone carries scars, Brie. I never forget that, especially when someone is being an ass towards me."

Brie nodded, both Ms. Clark and Mary instantly coming to mind. "I think it's only fair that you share your story, Boa."

He looked down at her untouched plate. "I think you should eat first."

While Brie was finishing up, Boa's Mistress walked in. Her eyes went straight to his groin and a sly smile formed on her lips. "Good boy."

He stood up and bowed to her. "What is your pleasure, Mistress?"

"We're leaving." When he walked up to her, the Domme caressed his flaccid cock, making it flaccid no more. "Come, pet. I think playtime is in order."

They left the room without acknowledging Brie. She smiled to herself, taking a bite of a ripe peach. Brie wiped the juices that rolled down her chin. It made her think of Boa pleasing his Mistress. There was no doubt he was in for a treat, having passed his Mistress's test.

Lea and the Subs

B rie sat alone in the room for a long time. She wondered what Sir was discussing with the trainers. Were they picking the new headmaster? She sighed, a fear nagging her; would there come a time when he resented the path his life had taken the day she knelt at his feet?

She was grateful for the distraction when she heard a group of girls chattering in the hallway. They stopped at the door just before it swung wide open. All the chattering stopped the moment they saw Brie.

She smiled self-consciously, feeling embarrassed, until a familiar voice rang out. "Oh my gosh! What are *you* doing here?"

Lea broke through the small crowd and rushed at her. She grabbed onto Brie and they jumped around in circles like schoolgirls. Brie couldn't stop smiling. It seemed like ages since she'd seen Lea, although it had only been a few days.

"You're supposed to be pleasing your Master, girl. You have no business being here!"

"Sir was called in and he asked me to join him."

One of the other girls huffed and the group moved as one to the table laden with food. Lea remained with Brie, bursting with numerous questions. "I wonder if Sir has special plans for you afterwards." She poked Brie in the ribs.

Brie swatted her away. "As a matter of fact, he does."

"Oh God, how is it, Brie? Having a Master… Sir, no less. I can't even imagine!"

Suddenly the entire room became silent. Apparently everybody wanted to know. "Sir is…" But she didn't want to share her experiences with everyone else so she finished by saying, "I'm seriously in love with him, Lea."

Her best friend squealed and hugged her again. "Every sub here wishes they were you, you know. Having the headmaster all to yourself… heck, I feel honored just to know you." Lea got on her knees and went to kiss Brie's feet.

Brie backed away, laughing. "Stop!"

An older-looking sub interrupted their silliness. "I'll be surprised if it lasts. Sir Davis was simply flattered by your youthful rashness."

Lea picked herself up from the floor and chided the woman. "Don't be like that, Rachael. Brie is one of the finest people I know, period. She and Sir are perfect for each other." Lea turned to Brie and smiled. "I knew it on that first day when he touched you. I felt the electricity between you, even then."

Brie quickly changed the subject, not wanting her love life open for discussion. "So, girl, what the heck are *you* doing here? I imagined you would take some time off before the new session started."

"Heck no! They are running us subbies through the paces. The Center has to make sure the Dominant training is top-notch. I've already had practice sessions with Baron and Tono."

Brie caught her breath when Lea mentioned Tono's name. She wanted to ask Lea how he'd seemed, but did not feel comfortable asking in front of the other subs. "Did they put you through the wringer?" she joked lightly.

"Oh, yeah. Baron teased me mercilessly with the swing. Had to beat me with a flogger to get my pussy to obey." Lea grinned and whispered, "I kinda cheated."

Brie laughed, imagining it in her head. "Did he complain what a difficult student you were?"

"No. But Master Nosh, the head trainer for the Dominant class, took me aside afterwards. He was less than amused."

One of the other subs broke in. "Lea is always pushing the boundaries."

Brie nodded, wrapping her arm around her high-spirited friend. "It's one of the things I love most about her."

Lea knew Brie well enough to know the question she could not ask. "As far as Tono," she began. Brie tried to hide her interest by picking up and chewing on a stray carrot. "He showed me his style of Kinbaku yesterday. I must say, he is a gentle teacher."

Brie looked into her eyes. "Yes, that is true."

"I found him a bit preoccupied," Lea continued, "but overall the experience was quite enjoyable."

A curly-haired blonde sub spoke up. "God, when he tells you to breathe with him I just want to die!"

Brie quickly changed the subject, not wanting to hear about their experiences with Tono. "So Lea, got any plans this weekend?"

Her face brightened up. "Why? Do you think we can get together? I would love that!"

"Yeah, I can show you my new crib. Maybe you can help me unpack my stuff."

Lea smiled wickedly. "You want me to invite Mary?"

Brie swatted her on the butt. "I can't believe you just went there, Lea! I retract my previous invite."

Lea pouted. "No… I'm sorry. I want to see your new place. Let me make it up to you. Why did the submissive cross the road?"

Brie shook her head.

"To get some hits."

"That was pathetic, Lea. You get no brownie points for that one."

"Okay, okay. If you are hankering for a spirited spanking, when your Dom tells you to look him in the eye, look at him cross-eyed."

Brie couldn't help it, she giggled at the stupid joke.

"There! See, I made you laugh. Now you have to let me come and help you unpack."

Several of the other subs chuckled in the background. Brie looked at them for sympathy. "Was that *really* worth a re-invite?"

Most smiled and voiced their support of Lea, but the oldest sub, the one who had expressed her doubts about Sir's choice, glared at her.

Lea jumped in. "There you go. They said yes, so now you have to let me come."

Brie was about to answer when the door opened. Sir appeared in the doorway, filling the small space with his commanding presence. Brie instantly jumped to attention, bowing her head.

His aura filled the room. The silence expanded until Sir asked, "How is the additional training going, Ms. Taylor?"

"Great, Sir."

"No issues?"

She hesitated for only a second before answering truthfully, "I do have my areas of weakness, Sir."

"As do we all," he replied generously before asking the group, "How are the rest of you faring?"

All of the girls answered at once, making it impossible to understand them. He chuckled lightly. "I see... I expect that each of you is putting forth your best effort."

Sir addressed Brie last. "Come, téa. I have something special for you."

She loved that he called her by his pet name in front of the others. It emphasized her new status. Brie shivered in pleasure when he placed his hand on the small of her back. "Good evening, ladies," he stated as he led Brie out of the room. She felt the jealous glares as she left, but she didn't mind—not one bit.

"Did you enjoy your time with the other subs, téa?"

She looked up at him and smiled. "It was good to see Lea, Master. I've missed her."

He chuckled. "You two are unusually close. It was pleasant to watch as you were training. I appreciated when you brought Mary into the fold."

Brie snorted in disgust.

"Do not be so quick to dismiss her," Sir stated as they walked down the hallway.

Brie tried to hide her resentment. "I will try not to, Master."

"Téa, try is not what I am asking from you."

She realized what he was demanding of her and re-formed her answer. "I will do my best, Master."

He smiled down at her. "See that you do."

Brie pressed her cheek against his muscular arm, grateful that he challenged her to think beyond herself. "Master?"

"Yes?"

"Would it be agreeable if Lea helped me unpack this weekend?"

He chuckled at the request. "I suspect the apartment will be filled with laughter. Yes, I find that agreeable."

"Thank you, Master." Brie squeezed his arm.

"Unfortunately, I have some unpleasant news, téa. Tonight I learned that Celestia, Marquis' sub, suffered a burst appendix while visiting her parents in Seattle. Marquis Gray has traveled to attend to her."

"Is she okay?" Brie hated to think of anything bad happening to the kind-hearted woman. Celestia had been with her the night of graduation and had proven to be quite a comfort during Mary's betrayal.

"She underwent emergency surgery and, from what I was told, she is recovering well. We will visit and provide a meal on their return."

She noticed that he was leading her towards the

kitchen area and her heart sank. The last thing she wanted was another cooking lesson.

Brie glanced up and saw a playful smirk on his lips. She dutifully slowed down as they approached the dreaded room forty-two, but Sir walked past it. So cooking was not on the schedule for the night!

"Normally, non-trainers are not allowed back here. However, while the classes are on hiatus, and in honor of my service, the staff has graciously offered me free run of the lower level."

There were still rooms Brie had yet to explore. Her heart raced faster the further down the hall they went. What was waiting for her behind those closed doors? Which one would it be?

Sir finally stopped at the end of the hall: They couldn't be any farther from the others—no one would hear her screams.

"Tonight's training begins."

As he opened the door, the butterflies began. What did Sir have planned for her this time?

The opposite side of the room was covered in mirrors. In the center was a small table and an apparatus that looked like a padded balance beam with a wooden pole attached to the head of it vertically.

"My own invention. It allows the sub control over the scene even when gagged. It also requires complete focus. Excellent for building a sub's endurance."

Brie stared at it, her eyes growing wider with each passing second.

Sir laughed warmly. "I am not planning to torture you. Where's the trust, my little sub?"

She glanced up at Sir apologetically. "Momentary lapse of reason, Master. I trust you completely."

He turned from her and muttered, "Maybe you shouldn't."

Her mouth fell open. Was he teasing her?

As Sir walked towards a cabinet in the far corner he instructed, "Undress completely and lie on your back. I want you to hold onto the pole with both hands."

Brie's whole body was trembling as she undid her corset and slipped out of her garter and hose. Sir already had her tense with anticipation. With his limitless experience, anything was possible tonight.

She gingerly lay down on the beam that looked to be about eight inches wide. Sir was right, she had to concentrate to balance her body on it. Brie bent her knees and placed her feet together to keep her balance. She then lifted her hands over her head too fast and nearly fell off the beam. She stopped to regain her composure before gripping the pole tightly with both hands.

Sir returned to her with a metal box in one hand and several items in the other. He looked down at her and smiled. "You must maintain your balance the entire time, téa. No matter what I do to you."

She nodded, looking up at him apprehensively, but unable to hide the excitement he inspired.

He put down the items on the table and proceeded to run his fingers over the length of her. Brie bit her lip, her skin tingling with the intensity of his touch, her nipples already painfully erect with need. He slipped his fingers between her legs. "As I expected. You enjoy the prospect of the unknown."

Sir picked up a piece of cloth. "Let's add to the experience. Lift your head and open your mouth." He quickly placed the cloth in her mouth and tied it. There was an added sense of vulnerability in not being able to speak.

"If I do anything you cannot handle, let go of the pole. The instant you do I will stop. Do you understand?"

She nodded with lustful eyes, watching his every move.

"Instead of a blindfold, I have something more romantic." He opened the white box and pulled out a huge red rose. He lifted it to his nose and smelled it, smiling at her. Then he put it under her nose and she breathed in its sweetness. He rubbed the soft petals against each nipple, then crushed the flower in his hand. "Close your eyes."

Brie did as he asked and felt the cold, velvet petals fall on her eyelids.

"A slight turn of your head and they will fall away. You are in complete control of this session, even though you are figuratively blind and bound."

Brie's chest was rising and falling rapidly. He hadn't even started yet and she was a delicious mess.

She heard him unsnap the lock on the metal box. He began riffling through, chuckling softly to himself. She heard him lay several items on the table, then shut the case.

"The human brain is a hotbed of imagination, capable of taking a simple stimulus and magnifying it many times greater than it is. I am going to leave you here, téa. Let your mind run wild."

She whimpered when she heard him walk away.

"This is my gift to you," he said before shutting the door.

Brie lay there on the thin length of wood smiling to herself. Sir certainly knew how to play her. Would he watch her from a camera, or had he rejoined the others while she contemplated what he would do?

Brie felt the tension of her stomach muscles as she remained stagnant on the balance beam. Luckily for her, the temperature of this room was pleasant and did not distract.

She imagined what he had placed on the table beside her. Was one of the items a Wartenberg wheel? Her skin instantly developed goosebumps at the mere thought. Could it be a variety of colored waxes? Brie's nipples ached at the thought of the hot wax rolling down them. Maybe he was planning something more intense. Were there clothespins or possibly nipple clamps on that table?

Would he do something she'd experienced before? *Probably not…*

When she heard him standing outside the door she held her breath, not wanting to lose her balance in the yearning he caused.

His Electric Touch

S ir entered the room quietly. She heard his footsteps as he walked to the far corner of the room. She silently questioned what he was doing until he volunteered the answer. "I do not care to have our private affairs recorded." So he was blinding the camera. It made the encounter seem much more personal, but also a little dangerous.

The distinct sound of his dress shoes as he approached made the butterflies in her stomach swarm. "Are you ready to begin, téa?"

Brie nodded slightly, so she did not displace the petals.

She heard him pick up something from the table and then buzzing filled the room.

The violet wand...

Brie wobbled on the beam as he drew near her. "We begin on the lowest setting." She felt the contact of the smooth glass as the sound of static filled the air and tiny electrical bursts tickled her stomach.

She giggled into her gag, loving the feel of it. Sir

moved it over her body, letting every area of her skin feel the stimulating effects of the device from her shoulders to her toes.

No wonder Lea likes it so much!

He disengaged for a moment and she heard the frequency of the wand increase. She whimpered, inadvertently jumping when it sparked against her skin. She had to quickly right herself or risk falling off as Sir glided it under the crease of her breasts before lightly touching the tips of her nipples. The current was still light enough to be tingling and she moaned into her gag, a gush of wetness flowing between her legs.

Sir slowly lifted her right leg and brushed the sole of her foot. Her pussy contracted in pleasure. With careful precision he lifted her other leg, holding her so that she did not fall as he caressed the sole of her left foot with the wand. She squealed into the gag when he slowly moved up her leg towards her mound. He brushed it lightly, a feeling of fizzy bubbles lingering after the pass.

Then he gently put her legs back down and let her regain her balance before he let go and turned off the wand. A few seconds later it was on again, the frequency of the wand much louder.

"Now this is where your concentration will come into play. The intention is not an exercise of endurance; it is about embracing a new stimulation. When it becomes unpleasant, I want you to let go of the pole."

Brie swallowed hard. So far it had been refreshingly ticklish. Nothing like the electric shocks she had been expecting. Now she was about to feel the bite of the device. The buzz itself was intimidating, but knowing that Sir had turned up the intensity had her quaking on the beam even before contact.

He had attached a different apparatus; it was not a smooth surface, but felt more like a pointed tip. It concentrated the electricity considerably. He ran it down the length of her torso. Brie really did jump this time and had to tighten her grip on the pole to steady herself. It made the hair on her skin stand, but the sensation reminded her more of a nail being dragged across her skin rather than the intense stinging she'd expected.

"Would you like to try another pass?" he asked with a lustful growl.

There was something incredibly sexy in the exchange of pleasure and pain with her Master. She nodded and the stinging burn traveled down the other side of her torso. Sir's fingers found their way between her legs and he groaned. "Your pussy speaks clearly." He played with her slippery clit, rubbing it sensuously.

Sir slipped his finger inside Brie and stroked her G-spot several times, teasing her before pulling out and slowly dragging the wand over her pelvis. She whimpered in pleasure. "Open your legs," he commanded.

With trepidation she placed the soles of her feet together and pulled her legs up carefully so that she did not lose her balance. Sir turned off the wand and replaced it with yet another apparatus, turning up the intensity even higher. She yelped as multiple tails from a metal flogger caressed her skin with little bites of electricity. Sir dragged it up her right thigh. The closer he got to her sex, the more her body contracted in fear and pleasure. He lifted the toy before he made contact with her mound and started with the left thigh. It took everything in Brie not to wiggle and twist. The idea of that metal flogger touching her clit had her squirming inside, but she lay still, taking deep breaths as it inched towards her pussy.

Just before it electrified her clit, he pulled it away, leaving her gasping into her gag. The violet wand went silent. She wondered what he planned next and was surprised when he said softly, "Lift your head an inch, but do not dislodge the petals."

She carefully lifted her head and he untied the gag. Brie put her head back down and lay there, trying to keep her breath calm as her pussy pulsated of its own accord.

The crackling noise of the violet wand started up again at a lower frequency. Sir leaned over her and she felt his warm breath on her lips. "I am electrified, my dear." She gasped in surprise as his mouth brushed against hers, making her lips tingle with electricity. His kiss was quick but he returned again, locking his lips with hers and causing her lips to burn with current. She whimpered when he pulled away. Sir leaned in for a third time. His energized tongue darted into her mouth and she cried out in surprised pleasure.

He broke the kiss and she felt his hands begin caressing her skin as they moved over her chest. Sir pinched her sensitive nipples, the electricity giving an extra bite.

"Oh, Master…" she purred. She squirmed under his touch and nearly fell off the beam because she refused to let go of the pole. Luckily Sir righted her, his laughter warm and deep.

His tingling fingers spread her thighs and then lightly caressed her mound. She cried out, overcome by the sensation of his electrified touch. Then he did the unthinkable... she felt his hot breath just before he licked her clit.

She froze.

Sir licked the length of her pussy the second time, his tongue burning with the current. She shook her head violently, the rose petals falling to the floor, but she refused to let go. She looked down and whimpered, swearing she could see sparks jump from his tongue. "Oh God, Sir, oh my God!"

He lifted his mouth from her pussy. "Your Master commands your orgasm."

Brie closed her eyes and willingly gave into the sensations his electrified tongue created. He pressed his tingling hands against her, holding her still as the fire built up inside her, his fluttering tongue shooting current with every pass. Brie screamed wildly when the orgasm finally crested and she came against his sparking tongue.

She was grateful for his support, still trembling even after the orgasm ended. Sir wiped his mouth with a smirk. "Electricity feels odd on the tongue, but is certainly worth the effect." He turned off the device and placed it on the table before undressing. His rigid cock left no doubt that the encounter had been equally arousing for him.

Sir picked up Brie in his arms and carried her over to the mirror, lifting her up. She instinctively wrapped her legs around his torso as he impaled her with his manhood. Her passionate screams continued when Sir powered his shaft into her. Brie slid up and down the glass as he fucked her against the mirrored wall, his labored breathing totally turning her on.

"I love being fucked by you, Master!"

He growled, clutching her thighs as he plowed in deeper. Sir let her have the full effect of his uninhibited passion. His fingers dug into her flesh as he bruised her with his powerful thrusts. All of it was welcomed, all of it wanted.

Master roared when he came. It was deliciously violent, taking her breath away in its ferocity. Sir buried his head in her neck afterwards, panting as he regained his composure. He slowly disengaged and lowered her to the floor. Sir kissed her on the lips. "My slut, my goddess."

He walked her over to a lounge chair in the corner and sat down. Brie crawled in his lap and curled up in his arms. They sat there for a long time in silence.

She smiled to herself, overcome with a feeling of intense love. "My Master, my Sir."

He chuckled. "I remember when you had the arrogance to call me that the second night of class."

She looked up and stated with conviction, "I think my spirit knew you, even before I understood."

He looked at her solemnly. "Yes, téa. I would agree."

She nestled up against him, loving the warmth of his embrace. "Thank you for finding me, Sir."

"Do you believe in fate?" he asked.

"No. I've always believed I make my own life what it is, Sir."

"I am undecided, myself," he answered, crushing her against his chest before letting her go. "Dress and clean the mirror with the spray you'll find in the cabinet."

She walked over to her clothes and dressed quickly, watching Sir meticulously clean the instruments as well as the beam.

They left the Center only after the room was returned to its original state. Several people greeted Sir as the two walked out, obviously pleased to see the ex-headmaster. It hurt Brie's heart. *He belongs here.*

On the way home, Sir asked, "What was the lesson for tonight?"

"I'm undecided, Sir. I learned tonight that pain can act as an aphrodisiac when applied by you. At the same time, being forced to balance on the beam helped me to control my reactions. Being in control like that improved my ability to govern my mental response."

He reached over and stroked her cheek tenderly. "Those are fine answers, téa."

The Haven

B rie received a text from Sir at noon the next day while working. *Tonight you shall be on display. To prepare yourself, every other hour you will remove a piece of clothing. You must send a photo of each piece. Begin now. Tell no one.*

Brie sighed nervously. He hadn't specified which pieces which meant the decision was up to her. She would have to be smart so that she wasn't left exposing herself by the end of her shift.

"Mr. Reynolds, can you watch the front for a moment? I need to use the bathroom."

Her boss looked at her strangely because she had just come off a break. "Sure, but make it quick."

"Yes, Mr. Reynolds." She hurried to the small bathroom, cursing because she had worn heels without stockings. Two items eliminated from her selection. With little time to think she went for the quickest, peeling off her panties. She took a picture with her phone and sent it to Sir. He immediately texted back. *Surprised by your first choice. It will be a long day of not bending over, my dear.* Brie had no place to put her panties, so she ran to the back of the store and stuffed them in her purse before returning to the front.

"Are you feeling okay?" Mr. Reynolds asked with genuine concern.

She blushed, quite aware of her lack of underwear as they conversed. "Yes, I feel much better. Thank you."

It was disconcerting working without her panties. She was conscious every time she moved, making sure to bend her knees so that she never exposed herself to the two trainees as she unpacked the cigarettes and helped to stock them.

When two o'clock rolled around, she asked Mr. Reynolds for another quick break.

"Again? What did you eat for lunch?"

"Sorry," she stammered, running to the bathroom. With ample time to think beforehand, she'd already decided on the next piece. Brie unbuckled the stylish little belt around her waist, taking a quick picture before rolling it up. After she hit send, Sir responded: *I do not consider that clothing, téa. No fashion accessories.*

Even though her time was short, she didn't want to disappoint Sir and quickly texted back. *Should I take off something else, Sir?*

Yes.

She unbuttoned her blouse and removed her lacy camisole. She dutifully took a pic and sent it to Sir. He did not return a text back. She worried for a second, but decided he must have been distracted by a business call or a visit from a client. Just as she was exiting the bathroom, Mr. Reynolds met her at the door. "Is everything all right, Brie? Do you need to go home?"

She held the camisole behind her back and stuttered, "No… no, sir. I'm just… It's…" She couldn't lie to her boss, but she didn't want to break Sir's explicit command either. The tension made her queasy, so she answered truthfully, "My stomach is a little upset."

He broke out in a huge paternal grin. "I'm not going to be a great-uncle, am I?"

She stared at him in shock. "No! Oh no, Mr. Reynolds."

He chuckled good-naturedly. "I'm just kidding, Brie. Have to admit, though, the look on your face was priceless."

She wasn't able to go to her purse, so she stuffed her camisole underneath the register. Brie definitely felt more exposed, knowing her white bra could now be seen through the thin material of her blouse, yet Sir's unique challenge also made her feel more alive than she'd ever felt at the tobacco shop.

At four, Brie was able to avoid asking Mr. Reynolds, who happened to be at the back door signing for newly arrived shipments. She went directly to Mike, instead. "Can you man the register until I get back?"

"I haven't learned how to work it yet," he protested.

"That's okay. If a customer comes, just tell them to wait. I won't be long."

"You need some Pepto-Bismol or something? I'm sure the old man must have some stashed somewhere."

Brie unintentionally snorted in laughter. "Ah, no…"

She closed the bathroom door and started giggling quietly to herself. In no time flat, she had her shirt off and her bra undone. She took a picture of the frilly thing and sent it to Sir.

His response was, *Now you will truly be on display.*

Brie balled up her bra and stuffed it behind the trashcan. With Mr. Reynolds in the back, she had no way to deposit it into her purse. Did Sir know how difficult this assignment was? *Probably...* He must have counted on the fact she was being challenged by the task.

She took a quick glance downward as she walked back up to the front. Sure enough, her pert nipples were poking through the thin blouse. She picked up a box and covered her chest with it when she addressed both trainees. "You guys should put out these tins. They go over on the end display by the door."

Laurel grinned, although Brie wasn't sure what she found so amusing. "Sure thing, princess."

Mike took the box from her and headed straight for the display. Brie took heart that Mr. Reynolds would have a fine replacement. It made leaving him much easier.

One of their regulars came in and asked for his normal carton of Salems. His eyes went straight for her chest as he handed her the money. Brie held her head a little higher to fight the urge to bolt.

She handed over his change, counting it out quickly. "And thank you for coming today, Mr. Abrams."

"Have a lovely day, Miss Bennett," he replied, tipping his hat.

She struggled with her feelings of embarrassment and feminine pride.

At ten before six, Mr. Reynolds came up to her.

"You must be anxious to get home. Go ahead and cut out a little early. Hopefully whatever ails you will have passed through your system by tomorrow." To his credit, his eyes never traveled from her face.

"It's really not necessary," Brie told him, feeling a little guilty.

"No, Brie. I insist."

She went to the back to gather her purse. Laurel met her there and, holding up Brie's bra, demanded, "What kind of game are you playing?"

She snatched it from the girl. Since she made a lousy liar she didn't even try, instead Brie answered with a simple, "It's none of your business."

"Hey, I'm just telling you there's no need to try so hard. Mike is an easy catch. He'll bed any girl who gives him the time of day."

"I'm not interested in Mike."

"Oh! So it's the old man you are gunning for."

Brie shook her head. "No, it is not like that. You have no idea what you are talking about."

Laurel laughed, obviously not believing her. "Hey, don't worry, chickie. Your secret's safe with me." She leaned in and whispered, "Personally, I think you should set your sights a little higher. That old man is married and doesn't make all that much."

Brie looked at her in disbelief. "Thanks for the advice, Laurel. I've got some, too. If you aren't going to work hard for Mr. Reynolds, quit now and save everyone the trouble. He deserves only the best."

As Brie walked away, Laurel sang out childishly, "Brie's got a crush on Mr. Reynolds…"

No doubt everyone in the tiny shop heard it, so Brie did the only thing she could. She held her head high, stuck out her chest with pride and walked out the doors with a smile on her lips. *People can think what they want.*

Sir was already home when she got there. He had her twirl in front of him so he could see the effects of his little game.

"You do look good without a bra, babygirl," he complimented.

He slipped his hand under her skirt and caressed her ass cheek before teasing her clit with his middle finger. "Bet they all wanted to do that," he growled before kissing her hard on the lips.

Brie closed her eyes, enjoying the magnetic pull of his dominance.

He withdrew abruptly to explain. "We will eat a light dinner before we head out. There are several people I have to meet with tonight at The Haven. But, rest assured, I also plan to scene with you while we are there."

Brie let out an excited squeak. Scening in public with Sir was a dream come true!

"While I talk with them, feel free to walk around and observe the other performances. Let me know if there are any that stimulate you."

"Sounds thrilling, Sir!"

His voice took on a serious tone. "I have also invited

someone to join us there to talk with you."

She wondered who it was, but noticed he wasn't providing a name. Sir did like to keep her guessing. He enjoyed trifling with her intense curiosity, knowing it was a characteristic she needed to gain control over.

After their simple meal, which Brie struggled to eat because of her elation, Sir directed her to dress. She skipped down the hallway to the bedroom and saw that he had laid out a black leather halter top, shiny vinyl skirt, and crotchless panties with cutouts in the back to nicely frame her heart-shaped ass. Instead of his preferred garters and hose, he had picked out thigh-high boots to go with the ensemble. It gave her a much edgier look, making her wonder what he had planned for their scene. Sir was capable of anything.

He nodded his approval when he saw her. He had changed into black slacks and a solid black button-up shirt. He still looked formal, but with an edgier feel that matched hers. "The exact look I was going for. You look absolutely edible, téa."

She basked under his lustful gaze. "Thank you, Master."

Brie was not surprised to see The Haven parking lot full when they drove up. It was the 'hot place' to be for those in the local BDSM community. She was feeling a little nervous, though. With Sir being such a prominent member, all eyes would be on them tonight. It was a lot of pressure, especially knowing there were many out there who found Brie unworthy of Sir's collar.

He chose you, she reminded herself as he opened the door and helped her out of the car. He pulled a black duffle bag out from the trunk and slung it over his shoulder before he escorted her to the club.

The sights and sounds of The Haven assaulted her senses. The place was packed and every alcove was already in use with various BDSM scenes being played out. Brie soon found herself surrounded as people crowded Sir, eager to talk to him. Brie kept her eyes on the floor, sensing that many of them were Doms. There was no way she was going to break protocol here.

After several minutes Sir insisted on moving along, guiding her with the back of his hand through the crowd. He walked her around the large center room, letting her glance at all the scenes available for her viewing pleasure in each alcove. She had to hide her shock when she saw Tono performing Kinbaku. A huge crowd had gathered to watch his artful performance. She had never admitted to anyone that Tono had been her choice at the Collaring Ceremony—up until the point she had met the eyes of his disapproving father as she had approached Tono with her collar. Brie had to force herself to remain calm, totally unprepared for meeting up with him.

Sir moved her onto the next scene. "You may enjoy watching Cat O' Nines. She is well known for her intense play."

Brie concentrated on the new scene, putting all her focus into it. The Domme's dramatic show fascinated Brie. The performance was enhanced by the powerful music she chose to accompany her work, a haunting melody with intense instrumentals.

Cat O' Nines' submissive was strapped to a St. Andrew's cross and already had red lash marks on his thighs and back.

She had just put down a cane and picked up a flogger with evil little knots on the end of each tail. She swung it in the air several times, showing the crowd her wicked-looking nine-tail before striking her submissive. His cry filled The Haven. Brie shifted uncomfortably, imagining that flogger making contact with her own skin.

The Domme played with her sub, striking several times and then cupping his ass or running her long nails between his legs. She continued like that, his cries of pleasure/pain building in intensity. Brie was horrified that she found it sexually arousing as welts appeared on his back.

There was a break in the action as Cat O' Nines unbound him and turned him around to face the crowd. His strong erection made it obvious that he thoroughly enjoyed his Mistress' attention. The Domme bound him again and began on his thighs, moving ever closer to his rigid cock. Brie was riveted.

"I must leave you, téa," Sir said quietly. "Feel free to walk around and observe. Once I am done with this meeting, you and I will enjoy our own scene."

Brie's heart raced as he walked away. *I hope it's a short meeting.* Just then, the masochistic sub roared out in pain, but Brie couldn't bear to look and headed back to Tono's scene instead.

The Asian Dom spent several minutes securing the girl's legs and then moved to her arms. He was very precise, needing her body to be perfectly supported balanced by the rope because he was preparing to lift her in the air. Long ropes attached to her body were already slipped through the large metal ring hanging in the air. However, it was easy to see the girl was nervous. Tono stopped what he was doing and wrapped his arms around her, whispering something in her ear.

The girl's face began to relax when she closed her eyes. Brie knew the sub was matching his breath and she found herself unconsciously doing the same. The instant she felt the harmony, Tono looked up and stared directly into her soul.

Brie stumbled backwards and then turned and ran to an alcove on the other side of the room. She pretended to watch a paddling session as she tried to regain her bearings. Brie hadn't expected the connection with Tono to remain as strong. She knew in her heart she must eliminate the emotional ties that bound her to the gentle Dom, but she had no idea how.

Toasted Brie

B rie had no idea how long she'd been standing there staring blankly at the scene, but she was brought back to life the moment she felt the warm breath of her Master on her neck. He growled in her ear, "Are you ready, téa?"

"Yes, my Sir."

He chuckled softly, kissing her on the top of her head. "What we are about to do will not hurt. I've been told by those I've scened with in the past that it is actually quite relaxing, but it will require your trust." He began guiding her through the multitudes, adding, "It is certain to draw a crowd."

"What are you going to do, Sir?"

He just smiled and said, "Trust me."

Brie sighed in nervous excitement. She loved the thrill of the unknown and Sir knew that—knew how it added a heightened sense of exhilaration. She practically skipped beside him as he took her to an empty alcove. This one was dark with midnight-blue walls and low lights. There was a table set at a slight incline in the center and the faint scent of cinnamon filled the small space.

"Take off all your clothes except your panties and lie face down on the table."

As Brie complied with his command, Sir began taking out items from the duffle bag. She glanced over to get a better idea of what he had planned for her, but the only item she recognized was a bottle labeled '70% Isopropyl Alcohol'.

Oh boy…

Brie lay down on the table and turned her head towards Sir, ignoring the crowd that was already gathering. It appeared that everyone wanted to see Sir play with his newly collared sub. She forced herself to take long, slow breaths to combat her nervousness. The last thing Sir took out from the duffle bag was a set of speakers which he plugged his phone into. He turned on music that featured a female with a lilting Celtic voice.

"We will begin by warming you up first," Sir said soothingly. He ran his fingers over her back and down her legs. As always, Sir's touch thrilled her. He ran his hands back up her legs and gave her framed little ass a light smack. Brie giggled, not expecting it.

She glanced at Sir and saw his smile as he began to caress with more pressure, causing her whole body to relax. Brie held her breath when he began tapping her skin, much the same way that Marquis Gray had when he flogged her. Brie quickly peeked at the items again, but noted there was no flogger.

"Curious, are we?" he murmured as his hands danced over her back and down her thighs. This time Sir slapped her buttocks twice with a much greater force so that the sound of it echoed in the small alcove.

Brie yelped. "A spanking session, Master?"

"No, I just love playing with your ass, téa." He winked at her as he smacked her again.

She heard several whispers and turned her head to see that the crowd had grown significantly in that short time. Sir moved away from her and came back with a brush. He began brushing her hair, binding it in a high ponytail so that it lay away from her shoulders. "We cannot have any hair in the way," he stated.

Sir went back to the duffle bag and pulled out a fire extinguisher. Brie shuddered involuntarily.

"Do you wish to continue, téa?" Sir asked.

She hesitated for just a second before answering. "Yes, Master."

"There is nothing to be frightened of."

"If she doesn't want to, I volunteer!" an uncouth submissive shouted from the crowd.

Sir ignored the unwelcomed offer, keeping his eyes solely on Brie. "In my opinion, fire is far more elegant than the violet wand. Truly a beautiful display." He peeled off her panties and asked her to keep her legs closed. "Cross your arms and lay your head down in a comfortable position. You must stay still at all times."

He lightly brushed her back with his fingers before walking over to the table. He poured the alcohol into a small container and put what looked like a large cotton swab into it. "The process is simple, téa. I will apply the alcohol and then light it. I will snuff out any lingering flames with my hand. You will not be burned. I have done this many times and am experienced in the art." He traced her backbone with his fingers before dragging the swab over her spine. "It feels cool initially as it evaporates," Sir lit a slow-burning match, "but that is about to change."

He leaned over and kissed her cheek, careful to keep the flame away from her. "Are you ready?"

"Yes, Master."

Sir tapped the flame on her back and intense heat raced up her back. Sir's hand swept the area in a fluid motion and the heat was gone. The crowd murmured their appreciation. It must have looked impressive.

"How was it?"

"Interesting. I would like to feel it again, Master."

"But of course…" Sir dragged the wet swab over her spine and tapped the flame against it. Again, the fire raced up her back. It was too fast to cause pain, although the heat was brief and concentrated. Sir swept the flames away before they burned her skin.

"I believe your ass is craving a little attention, téa."

Brie bit her lip as he caressed both cheeks with his free hand. Where his hand touched, the alcohol soon followed.

"I always said you had a hot ass." The crowd chuckled as he tapped her right cheek with the match and spanked it out with his hand. Then he moved to the left cheek, slapping that one several times just for fun after the flames went out.

Brie closed her eyes as Sir explored her body with the flames. Always his caress came before the cool of the liquid and the burn of the heat. He had been right; it was relaxing and it was made all that more pleasant because of the abundant touching it required.

"Now we will ramp it up a notch," he announced to the crowd. Brie turned in time to see Sir take a swig from another cup on the table just before a fireball shot from his lips up into the air.

People broke out in enthusiastic applause. Brie glanced over and saw that the crowd was huge now. Sir rinsed his mouth out with water before leaning down and giving Brie a kiss on the lips. "Turn over, téa."

She turned herself onto her back so that she was facing Sir. The fire in his hand danced in the reflection of his eyes, giving him an almost sinister look. "Now you can witness the beauty of the flames."

Sir blew out the match and put it back on the table. Like he had done for her back, he caressed her skin, warming it up before the fire play ensued, but this time he interspersed the caresses with gentle kisses all over her body. Brie purred silently. Could there be anything better than this?

He turned up the volume, letting the lilting Celtic melody set the scene. Then he traced a line on her thigh before following it with the alcohol. Sir lit the match and said with a grin, "Toasted Brie," just before he tapped the flame on her thigh and the fire raced up her leg.

Brie gasped in surprise. It was exhilarating to actually see the flame as she felt its heat. "Oh, Sir…"

"Do you like, téa?"

She looked into his flaming eyes. "Very much, Master."

"My fiery goddess," he growled as he caressed her

other thigh. Brie held her breath as she watched him set fire to her skin. The flames danced upon her body before he swept them away. It was extremely sensual on a level she had not experienced before. She could feel the excitement of the crowd as they watched Sir skillfully control the fire to the graceful rhythm of the music.

He leaned forward and whispered in her ear, "This may feel a little hotter, my dear. Nipples are sensitive bits."

She looked at him in fear. "Master…"

He smiled down at her, his eyes blazing orange. "Do you trust me?"

She did not hesitate this time. "Completely, Master."

"As it should be."

Brie noticed that Sir picked up a towel and soaked it with water before announcing to the crowd. "You know you have a superior sub when she will let you do this."

He swirled the cotton tip over her right nipple, leaving only a trace of the fuel. He put it down and returned to her. With a sinuous movement, he tapped the flame on the tip of her erect nipple and Brie cried out as the fire consumed it. In an instant Sir swept the flame away with the damp towel and his warm mouth had encased her nipple. He sucked hard as the crowd went wild.

When he pulled away, Brie whimpered in protest, wanting more.

"Would you like me to light the other one?" he asked, his voice hoarse with desire.

"Please, Master."

He repeated the performance, letting it burn on her left nipple a second longer. Brie's pussy contracted in pleasure when she felt the coolness of the towel and the warmth of his lips as they landed on her nipple. Sir reached between her legs. "So wet," he murmured as he kissed her, stroking her clit gently with his finger.

This time when he pulled away, her pussy was pulsing with need. Instead of relieving the ache, Sir placed a large blanket over her. He kissed her forehead. "Allow yourself to enjoy the aftereffects of fire play, téa."

Sir began cleaning the area, but continually came back to touch and whisper his praise of her as he gave her sips of water. People began to disperse, but there were a few who remained. Brie was certain they were subs who wished that they could trade places with her.

Brie stared at the ceiling and smiled. *Luckiest sub in the world.*

A Desperate Move

O nce Sir was assured Brie was fine to move about, he informed her that he had one last meeting to attend. "I do not care for leaving you so soon, téa. You may continue to observe the other scenes or retire in the back to be alone for a few minutes." He tilted her chin up and graced her with his stunning smile. "I admire your trust in me, little sub. It was beautiful to witness."

"You have earned my trust, Master. I would do anything you ask."

"Then I ask that you trust your natural instinct, téa." He put his hand gently on her chest. "If you ever feel a checking in your spirit telling you to stop, I expect you to honor it."

She looked into his magnetic eyes. "I will, Master. I promise."

He nodded. "Good."

Sir turned her around and smacked her on the ass. "Now, go off and find something you want Master to try."

She glanced back at him and grinned. "If it pleases

you, Sir."

Brie wandered through the crowds searching for something unusual, something that called to her pussy—so to speak.

"Brie..."

She peered to her left and saw Faelan standing beside her. Her heart jumped into her throat. "Go away!"

"I won't touch you and I won't stop you if you walk away, but I need you to hear me out."

Brie backed away, looking around desperately for Sir, but he was nowhere in sight. "Mr. Wallace, I got in serious trouble the last time I talked to you."

"You weren't the only one, Brie, and I am sorry. I should have talked to Davis first as per protocol. However, I did get permission to talk with you tonight in this public area. There's no reason to be concerned."

Brie scanned the crowd again, unsure if it was really okay to talk to him, but then she remembered Master saying that he wanted her to meet with someone tonight. Faelan interrupted her thoughts, stating, "Brie, you need to listen. I *need* you to understand."

She frowned, not understanding what possible good it could do. However, Sir wanted her to speak with him so it was her duty to listen. "Understand what, Mr. Wallace? Nothing you say can change what's transpired. I don't see how talking will help either of us." She stared at the floor, unsure where to look in a situation like this.

"Brie, I'm sorry for any pain I've caused you." Faelan's voice caught. "But you should know that you've changed my life. Given me direction and hope. I can't stand the thought of you not knowing the significance of what you have done or how I feel about you."

She looked up into his soulful blue eyes. "Okay, I forgive you."

He shook his head violently. "No, I will not be satisfied until you understand."

Brie crossed her arms, sighing irritably. "Fine! You said you didn't have relations with Mary. I believe you, but I will never understand why you didn't tell me that night. Why did you avoid the question and act like I was in the wrong for questioning you about it?"

"Because you were wrong to question me. It was the same as saying you didn't trust me. I don't know Mary, why would I jeopardize *us*, what *we* had, for a stranger? It upset me that you understood me so little."

She frowned. "But it wasn't just that. During the interview, you were so flippant with your answers, as if you didn't care enough to take the interview seriously—or me for that matter."

"I thought you were mine," he answered candidly. "I thought the interview was simply a formality for us." He moved to touch her, but stopped himself. "You and I... we are meant for each other. Two people cut from the same cloth. I knew it when I met you. Damn it, Brie! I thought you felt the same way."

She looked at him with renewed sympathy, but stuck to her guns. "You seemed so overconfident that night, like I was more of a conquest, not someone you actually cared for. And then the way you acted with Mary..."

"I fucked up that night, blossom. I admit that. But you need to know where I've been, why you mean so much to me."

Faelan's potential confession frightened her. Brie glanced around again, searching for Sir in the crowd.

He spoke in a low tone so that others could not hear. "I killed someone, blossom." She didn't believe what she'd just heard, so she inched closer to hear him more clearly. "At sixteen, I killed a boy my age while driving home at night. I was lighting a cigarette and the match fell. I ran a red light, but didn't know it until I looked up and saw the other car just before I crashed into it. The poor kid never had a chance." He stopped, taking a ragged breath.

Brie said nothing, but in her head she imagined the other kid, eyes wide in horror as his death raced towards him, no way out.

"It should have been me. I should have been the one to die that night. No way should that kid have paid for my carelessness."

"That's so awful..." she said sorrowfully.

His blue eyes had a haunted look when he spoke. "I will never forget the terror on his face in the glare of the headlights or the sound at impact." He shuddered and abruptly turned away from her.

Brie was tempted to touch his shoulder in order to comfort him, but she resisted the urge, knowing it could be misconstrued by others.

When Faelan faced her again, he'd regained his composure. "Brie, I have lived every day since then imprisoned in a wall of guilt and self-hatred. It ruined any chance at a normal life and I often wished I was dead. Until you happened."

She shook her head. "I didn't do anything."

He smiled at her. "The day you fell into my arms I felt a spark of life, a connection. Then when I saw you at the beach and realized what you were training to be, everything fell into place. I *knew* I was meant to be your Dom and I was single-minded in my quest to win you over. Even Davis agreed. Why else would he allow me to join the training, take me under his wing and give me additional lessons? Why?"

"I don't know. I can't answer that."

"Of course you can't," he said in a reasonable voice. "Because you and I are meant to be together."

"No! I did my best not to lead you on," she protested.

"But it made me want you all the more. You felt the chemistry between us, you can't deny it."

"Chemistry does not equal love—"

"We hardly had any time together, Brie. I am certain if we spent quality time together, you would feel differently."

Brie growled in frustration. "You're not thinking straight. I have already made my decision. There is no going back now. That's the problem. You're so sure about things that you never *listen*."

He held up his hands in agreement. "Okay. You're right. Go ahead, it's your turn to talk. I'm listening."

Brie knew her words would not be easy for Faelan to hear, but she needed to be completely honest with him. "Yes, it's true. I felt an attraction towards you, but my heart was already taken. Even I didn't realize how completely until the night of the ceremony."

"You said 'felt' as if in the past. Are you saying you

don't feel attracted to me now? Can you honestly say that?" he insisted.

"There you go again… *listen* to me, Mr. Wallace. I am in love with someone else. I have already chosen the man I will serve. I'm sorry about what happened to you in the past, truly I am. But it doesn't change anything. You have to move on."

He shook his head and smiled sadly. "Brie, you and I never had time to get to know each other on a personal level. I want that. I want you to know the real me. Reject me if you must, but do it with a full understanding of who I am. Do not base it on a few encounters during a couple of scenes."

The vulnerability he was displaying physically hurt Brie. She had never suspected the depth of his feelings. It made what she had to do so much harder.

Brie took a deep breath before beginning. "I believe that everything that happened on graduation night—"

Then she heard *his* voice behind her. "What are you doing, téa?" Sir's tone was controlled, but accusatory.

Brie felt her stomach drop, realizing she had made a terrible mistake. "Mr. Wallace… said you gave him permission to speak with me. I thought he was the one I was supposed to meet with tonight, Master."

Sir's reply was simple and direct. "Have I given you permission to speak to Mr. Wallace?"

Brie's lip trembled. "No, Master."

Sir faced Faelan and shot his next words at him. "Mr. Wallace, you have ignored my edict. I directed you not to speak with my submissive. The fact you had the audacity to lie to her on top of it illustrates your lack of maturity and decorum. Leave now. But let me be perfectly clear, you are not to communicate with Miss Bennett or come within fifty yards of her. Do you understand?"

The entire club had become silent as the scene played out between the three of them. The crowd respectfully watched the confrontation. Faelan glanced around, possibly looking for supporters among the group, but found none. He nodded curtly to Sir, but his eyes traveled back to Brie. "Don't reject me, blossom. Not without getting to know me first."

"That's it!" Sir roared. He gestured to the manager of the club and two staff members surrounded Faelan, taking hold of his arms and physically forcing him out of the club.

As he was being dragged out, Faelan yelled, "I love you, Brie! I love you more than he ever could. You have to give me a chance. We're meant for each other…"

Sir's neck pulsed with rage, but he did not respond. Instead, he turned his attention back on her. "You were told *not* to speak to Mr. Wallace."

It was humiliating having the entire club witness her mistake, but Brie was far more crushed having failed Sir a second time. Would he disown her now?

She wanted to fall at his feet and beg forgiveness, but it would only anger him further. So she stated with conviction, "I was misled, Sir. I will not let that happen again."

He snarled, "It is obvious that the boy is in need of correction." Sir looked around and motioned the club owner to him. "Until Mr. Wallace learns respect, he has no business being amongst others in the community."

"Understood, Sir Davis. You don't have to worry about seeing his face around here again."

Brie couldn't help hearing the discontented sighs of several of the submissives around her. Faelan was a favorite among the eligible subs.

"It's time I teach Mr. Wallace I mean business," Sir announced to the club owner before leaving Brie's side and heading out the door. Several people tried to follow after him, but the owner shooed them away. "Nothing to see here, folks. Go back to what you were doing."

A sub next to Brie muttered, "God, she is such a bitch! Just *had* to ruin it for the rest of us. Already has Sir and now she's taken away Faelan from us."

Brie glanced over, half-expecting to see Mary, but it was a short-haired blonde who stuck her tongue out at her.

What had started out as the perfect evening had quickly deteriorated into a humiliating spectacle. She wanted to escape, *needed* to escape from the resentful stares of the submissives surrounding her and the utter disgrace she felt. However, Brie remained where she was, staring blankly at the scene before her, wondering what was going on between Sir and Faelan. The Domme was enthusiastically whacking the jiggling buttocks of her submissive with a wooden paddle. The crack of the paddle broke through Brie's anguish, helping her not to cry. *Just concentrate on them*, Brie commanded herself.

Until she overheard, "Do you think he will publicly disown her when he returns?"

Her greatest fear voiced out loud ruined her resolve. Tears streamed down her face as she ran through the crowds to the back of the club, seeking out a private room. Once found, she collapsed on a chair, wiping away her tears. *Sir is a good Master. He will not disown me. He won't...*

"Brie, are you okay?"

She looked up to see Tono standing in the doorway.

"What are you doing here?" She could just imagine Sir walking in on her talking with Tono. "Go away!" Then she remembered who she was talking to and corrected herself, begging him. "Please, Tono. Please go away."

He left without further question. A short time later, Sir strode into the room. Brie fell to her knees, "Sir, I did not mean to disobey. I'm sorry." She bowed her head to the floor, swallowing her tears.

"Stand up, Brie."

She slowly got on her feet, but kept her head lowered.

"Look at me."

Brie bravely looked up and was greeted with a grave expression, but she took heart at the tender look in his eye.

"I understand why this happened."

A single tear fell from her cheek.

"There is no need for tears. I did say you were to meet with someone tonight." He brushed the wetness from her cheek, chuckling lightly. "Tono said you ordered him away."

Brie nodded, unsure why that was funny, but she was relieved to see his smile.

"*He* was the one I wanted you to speak with tonight."

"I didn't know, Sir."

"No, you did not. It is fortunate that you chose not to speak with Tono due to that very fact. You are learning, téa." He leaned down and kissed her lightly on the lips.

He sat down on the couch and Brie naturally knelt down at his feet, laying her cheek against his strong thigh. Once Sir touched her, all worry evaporated.

"Brie, I know you have lingering feelings for Tono and I am not threatened by them. He is a mature Dom who respects your decision." The tone of Sir's voice softened as he stroked her hair. "I know you, téa. I understand that you suffer from guilt. I'd hoped tonight your heart would be eased by speaking with him directly."

His hand stopped mid-pet. "Naturally, I did not foresee Wallace's breach of protocol, but that will end." Sir lifted her chin to look her in the eye. "If he comes anywhere near you again, you are to ignore him and leave. If he dares to follow you, seek protection from the nearest person you trust. Although we reached an understanding tonight, I am not entirely convinced he will leave you alone. He admitted to me he has the misguided hope that he can still win you over, even though you are collared. Until he understands that reality no longer exists, he will remain a problem."

"Sir, I'm—"

"I do not blame you, do not apologize again. But I want to know what he shared with you tonight."

"He told me about the accident."

"Yes. A terrible circumstance indeed, but do not let it color your feelings towards him. One must come to terms with one's past to be effective as a Dominant. It should never be used to garnish sympathy from a sub."

Brie was hesitant to voice the one thing that Faelan had stated the first time he'd cornered her that still played in her mind. "Sir, he claimed I am his reason."

Sir shook his head in disbelief. "He is a fool to put that burden on another. I understand his desperation having been there once, but it is still no excuse. Wallace will be good to no one until he works through his demons."

It was so easy to be open with Sir that she shared her biggest fear. "I am afraid Mr. Wallace will turn away from his natural talent. He has often said we were cut from the same cloth and in a way, I agree with him. He didn't realize who he was until he met me." She looked up at her Master. "Well, Sir, I didn't realize who I was until I met you."

"The difference, babygirl, is that you have not been solely dependent on me. I am certain that if I had truly turned you away at the Collaring Ceremony, you would have found another. I cannot imagine you stalking me out of desperation, hoping to win my affections. You are confident in who you are. Wallace isn't there yet."

Brie looked down at the floor, a twinge of fear stabbing her in the gut. "What if he doesn't recover from this, Sir?"

"You are not responsible for the world, Brie. Wallace is stronger than you think and the call of dominance will not let him rest. At this point he sees you as his, but he will come to realize you were only a stepping stone to his true mate."

Sir's words brought comfort to Brie's soul. "Thank you, Master."

"The challenge is getting him to see beyond his own desires so that he can embrace the future." He cupped her chin. "However, that is *not* your job. You will only hinder his growth if you intervene in any way."

"I understand, Sir."

They were silent for several minutes. Brie basked in her Master's soothing caress. It comforted her that he did not react to Faelan with irrational jealousy. In all things, Sir remained the teacher, seeking the best conclusion for all the individuals involved.

"Now Tono is a different story," Sir stated.

Brie looked up at him questioningly.

"Tono is a good man. I have nothing but respect for him as a person and a Dom. I believe it would be in the best interests of both of you to sit down and discuss what happened the night of the ceremony."

"If it pleases you, Sir," she answered doubtfully.

"It is easy to underestimate the power of closure. I have found that loose ends tend to cause needless doubt and pain."

Despite his bravado, Brie wondered if it would hurt Sir on some level to see her with Tono.

He laughed under his breath. "If it is my jealousy you are worried about, téa, let me assure you that is not a concern. I have faith in your commitment. You asked to be collared of your own free will, despite the risk of rejection. I am confident in your love, just as you should be confident in mine. I am a condor, my dear."

Brie was unsure what the reference meant. Condors were not handsome birds and, as far as she knew, they were carrion eaters. Not romantic in the least, but she was reluctant to ask because of the look of tenderness he bestowed on her. She would definitely have to google it.

Thane

"I think it would be best if we leave through the back," Sir advised. "Your discussion with Tono will have to wait."

"Yes, Sir." She was grateful to be leaving, feeling far too emotionally raw to deal with any more drama.

"Everything you feel is written on your face." He had said the same thing the night he'd put the protection collar around her neck the second day of class.

"I am grateful you can read me so well, Sir. It eases my mind, even though it alarms me."

He chuckled softly. "It should. You can hide nothing from your Master." Sir stood up and held out his hand. She gracefully rose to her feet and took hold of his arm as he guided her through the back hallways.

The night was warm. Brie found it pleasant strolling with Master in the dark, loving the sound of his confident stride on the pavement. As they rounded the front of the building, Sir stopped and commanded, "You will walk to the car and get in. Do not look anywhere but straight ahead."

He nudged her towards the car while he stayed back and growled at Fealan, "Why are you still here?"

"Brie!" Faelan called out.

Brie hurried her steps, her eyes fixed desperately on the car. *Do not look, do not look back...* she commanded herself.

"Blossom, I'll wait as long as it takes to prove the depth of my love for you."

Sir's voice was like ice. "You were told to leave, Mr. Wallace. I am dialing the police as we speak."

Brie made it to the car and slipped into the seat, shutting the door. She heard their heated exchange, but could not make out the words. Sir eventually got into the car, slamming the door.

He said nothing until they were close to his apartment. "He's a stubborn cuss, I'll give him that much."

Brie didn't say anything as they walked into the highrise, although she nodded to the doorman when Sir didn't respond to the man's greeting.

Faelan's persistence astonished Brie and it did not help to serve his cause. By not respecting Sir's position, he was only making a fool of himself and tarnishing his reputation as well as that of the school. Brie did not want that for Faelan, especially after all he had suffered.

"Téa, make me a martini," Sir said when they entered the apartment.

She had watched him enough times to feel confident imitating the process. She doubted her martini would compare to his, but she smiled when she shook the drink vigorously. *Shaken, not stirred, Sir.*

He was on the phone the entire time she made the

drinks. She walked up to him, holding the martini up, careful not to spill. Sir smiled as he took it from her, but did not stop his conversation on the phone. "Yes, I think it is for the best. I am glad you are in agreement."

Brie went back to the kitchen to retrieve her drink. It had to be Faelan he was discussing, but who was he talking to and what was he planning? She knew Sir would not put up with his latest actions, but she desperately hoped that Faelan would not be banished from the BDSM community.

She returned to stand next to her Master, sipping her first attempt at a martini. It was definitely not as good as Sir's.

"Hard to believe, I know."

Sir chuckled at whatever was said by the caller. He clinked glasses with Brie and took a sip. "No, I agree. However, you have my expectation set unrealistically high. Do not disappoint me." He took another drink, his face suddenly becoming solemn. "Affirmative. There are times when it takes an extreme catalyst to force change."

Brie was certain he was talking about Faelan now.

"I need to make arrangements. Expect a call in a couple of days." He paused, and then the smile returned to his face. He looked down at Brie. "That would be a definite yes."

Sir tossed the phone on the couch and said, "I am not a man who will be pushed. However, when an opportunity presents itself, I'm not foolish enough to ignore it." He said no more, but seemed much more relaxed after the phone call. She breathed a sigh of relief, taking another sip of her mediocre martini.

He nodded towards the Tantra chair. "Your Master is feeling amorous. Strip down, téa, but leave the boots on tonight."

Brie set her drink on a side table and took off her clothes sensually for her Master. She couldn't help noticing the outline of Sir's erection straining against his pants. She swayed her hips in a seductive manner to entice him further as she ran her hands down her thighs and over the smooth black leather of her boots.

Both had been aroused by the fire play they'd engaged in earlier, but neither had experienced release. It heightened Brie's sense of arousal now.

"Undress me," he commanded.

Brie smiled as she began unbuttoning his shirt, feeling the familiar stirring in her loins as she exposed his muscular chest. She wanted to run her hands over his dark chest hair, but followed his order and undid his leather belt next. It excited her that Sir was observing her as she undressed him.

She unzipped his pants and pulled them down, helping him out of each leg. Brie looked up at him from the floor, in awe of his commanding masculinity.

"Stay." Sir left her, walking back to his bedroom and returning with a blanket. He moved over to the Tantra chair and lay down, placing the blanket on the floor. He looked at her and ordered lustfully, "Come."

The butterflies started as she approached him, moving with catlike grace towards her Master. He offered his hand for balance as she lifted her leg and positioned herself over his shaft. Brie closed her eyes as she lowered herself on his rigid member, letting out a moan of pleasure when he grabbed her hips and forced himself inside her depths. He then took the blanket and threw it over her shoulders, covering them both.

In that warm embrace he kissed Brie, moving her tight pussy up and down his shaft slowly, sensually. "I wanted to take you at The Haven, but I resisted knowing it would be far more satisfying to wait." Sir did not kiss her wildly. Instead, he was tender and controlled. Not at all what she was expecting. It caused her to slow down and enjoy the teasing way his tongue played across her lips.

"I want you to touch yourself."

Brie reached beneath the blanket and played with her wet clit. She became a little more adventurous and felt the rim of her opening as Sir pushed his cock in and out of her swollen lips. Apparently it turned him on as well because Sir groaned.

His pleasure encouraged her to continue exploring with her fingers, playing with his shaft as she felt their physical connection. Eventually, he took her hand and lifted it to his lips, licking her fingers. It was such an intimate gesture, a soft whimper escaped Brie's lips.

He smiled, placing both of her hands on his chest as he continued to pump his shaft into her with unhurried movements. Brie tilted her hips and rolled with each thrust. They both cried out at the intensity of the new angle. He pressed further into her then, each stroke rubbing her clit as he cradled her ass and maximized his slow lovemaking.

Brie was surprised when Sir stopped and caressed

her face. He pulled her close and breathed into her ear. "I love you, Brie."

Those words had power over her. She closed her eyes, hardly able to breathe. "I love you, Sir," she whispered.

"Say that again, but call me by my name."

She stopped her movements and gazed deep into his eyes. "I love you, Thane."

He crushed her to him, kissing her passionately—both seeking to meld into one another. It was like a dream, their open emotion mixed into the physical act of making love. In that moment there was no Dom, only a man desperately in love with his woman.

When he came, Brie threw back her head and shouted, "Yes, Thane, yes!"

He stopped in the middle of his release so she could feel the pulsing of his orgasm. With his shaft still throbbing inside her, he reached between her legs and caressed her to a sweet climax. She collapsed on his torso afterwards, totally and utterly in love with the man.

He tucked the blanket around her gently. "I find myself in new territory, téa."

She smiled, her cheek pressed against his chest. "How so, Master?"

He paused. "Love is a challenge for me."

She lay there listening to his heartbeat. Finally, she braved the question she was dying to ask. "Am I your first, Sir?"

He said nothing, but squeezed her against his chest in response.

She didn't know why, but she suddenly blurted, "I promise to be gentle, Sir."

He pinched her ass playfully. "Be gentle... who do you think you are? You deserve to be punished for that."

She propped herself on his chest, grinning at him. "I wish everyone could be this happy."

She saw a flicker of sadness in his eyes when he answered, "Yes. Wouldn't that be ideal?" She wondered if the pained look had something to do with his father. The last thing she wanted was to lose this feeling of closeness. She kissed his shoulder lovingly before laying her head against it. They stayed in that position for a long time, staring at the lights of the city under the warmth of his blanket.

"I'm so happy, Sir. I never want this moment to end."

His voice rumbled in his chest. "Never wish for stagnancy, Brie. It is important to grow—in our case, to grow together. You may be interested to know that I have just arranged an overseas trip for the two of us."

She lifted her head. "Overseas, Sir?"

"Yes. It will give Wallace time to regain his senses with you nowhere in reach."

She couldn't hide her excitement. "Wow, I've never traveled out of the country before, Sir!"

He looked at her questioningly. "Do you have a passport?"

Brie shook her head.

"No matter, we leave in a week which will allow you time to finish up at the shop and get your passport in order."

"I can't believe it! Where are we going? I hope it is someplace exotic…"

His laughter was low and tantalizing. "I'm unsure if destination matters. We won't be getting out much, my dear."

She bit her lip to stop from giggling. It sounded a lot like a honeymoon. The idea of traveling with Sir as his partner made her weak inside.

"Brie, there is something that concerns me."

Her bliss instantly disappeared. "What is that, Sir?"

"You have never spoken of your parents."

Brie let out a sigh of relief. "Well, there's really not much to say. They're in Nebraska and live quite ordinary lives, Sir."

"Tell me about them."

She smiled, glad his request was something so simple. "Well, my dad's name is Bill and he's forty-three. My mom's name is Marcy and she's a year younger." He looked at her expectantly, so she continued. "Dad works as an accountant these days and Mom has been a preschool teacher for years. Really, that's about it, Sir."

"Do they know about us?"

She hesitated. "No, Sir."

"Is there a reason?"

Brie looked at him earnestly. "They wouldn't understand, Sir."

"We don't have to detail our sex lives, Brie. However, they should know that you are in a committed relationship."

She gave him an uneasy smile. "Sir, I don't know how my parents will take the news that you are only ten years younger than my dad."

"Whether they like it or not, they should be told. It is irresponsible to keep them in the dark."

Brie lowered her eyes, knowing he was right but dreading the confrontation. She nodded her acquiescence.

"I will set up a layover so that I can meet with them in person before we leave the country. Hopefully it will help ease their minds about us."

She kissed him tenderly on the lips. "I love that you are so thoughtful, Sir."

"I expect you to call your parents tomorrow and explain that we have been seeing each other for the last six weeks. Do not lie, but keep the details simple." He looked down at her with a half-smile that made her heart flip-flop. "I am interested in meeting your parents, téa."

"They're good people, Sir, but old-fashioned and fairly ordinary."

"Your parents raised an exceptional daughter. That makes them interesting to me."

Brie blushed and kissed him again. She'd already decided not to mention his age when she talked to them on the phone. She wanted her mother and father to judge Sir on his own merits, not any preconceived ideas they might hold. Surely once they met him in person they would see what an incredible man he was.

Sir stirred underneath her. "Let's finish our martinis in the bedroom." He got up and handed Brie her drink with a wicked little grin, clinking his glass against hers. "There are a few things I want to teach you before we head off to Russia."

Brie followed him into the bedroom, shaking her head in disbelief. *Sir and Rytsar together?* Just the mere thought of it made her lightheaded and weak.

Can Brie survive another encounter with
the sexy Russian?

Find out as she heads to foreign lands in *Try Me*.

Buy the next in the series:

#1 (Teach Me)   #2 (Love Me)   #3 (Catch Me)

#4 (Try Me)   #5 (Protect Me)

Brie's Submission series:

Teach Me #1
Love Me #2
Catch Me #3
Try Me #4
Protect Me #5
Hold Me #6
Surprise Me #7
Trust Me #8
Claim Me #9

You can find Red on:
Twitter: @redphoenix69
Website: RedPhoenix69.com
Facebook: RedPhoenix69

 ****Keep up to date with the newest release of Brie by signing up for Red Phoenix's newsletter:
redphoenix69.com/newsletter-signup****

Red Phoenix is the author of:

Blissfully Undone
* Available in eBook and paperback
(Snowy Fun—Two people find themselves snowbound in a cabin where hidden love can flourish, taking one couple on a sensual journey into ménage à trois)

His Scottish Pet: Dom of the Ages
* Available in eBook and paperback
Audio Book: *His Scottish Pet: Dom of the Ages*
(Scottish Dom—A sexy Dom escapes to Scotland in the late 1400s. He encounters a waif who has the potential to free him from his tragic curse)

The Erotic Love Story of Amy and Troy
* Available in eBook and paperback
(Sexual Adventures—True love reigns, but fate continually throws Troy and Amy into the arms of others)

eBooks

Varick: The Reckoning

(Savory Vampire—A dark, sexy vampire story. The hero navigates the dangerous world he has been thrust into with lusty passion and a pure heart)

Keeper of the Wolf Clan (Keeper of Wolves, #1)

(Sexual Secrets—A virginal werewolf must act as the clan's mysterious Keeper)

The Keeper Finds Her Mate (Keeper of Wolves, #2)

(Second Chances—A young she-wolf must choose between old ties or new beginnings)

The Keeper Unites the Alphas (Keeper of Wolves, #3)

(Serious Consequences—The young she-wolf is captured by the rival clan)

Boxed Set: Keeper of Wolves Series (Books 1-3)

(Surprising Secrets—A secret so shocking it will rock Layla's world. The young she-wolf is put in a position of being able to save her werewolf clan or becoming the reason for its destruction)

Socrates Inspires Cherry to Blossom

(Satisfying Surrender—a mature and curvaceous woman
becomes fascinated by an online Dom who has much to
teach her)

By the Light of the Scottish Moon

(Saving Love—Two lost souls, the Moon, a werewolf
and a death wish…)

In 9 Days

(Sweet Romance—A young girl falls in love with the new
student, nicknamed 'the Freak')

---

9 Days and Counting

(Sacrificial Love—The sequel to In 9 Days delves into
the emotional reunion of two longtime lovers)

And Then He Saved Me

(Saving Tenderness—When a young girl tries to kill
herself, a man of great character intervenes with a love
that heals)

Play With Me at Noon

(Seeking Fulfillment—A desperate wife lives out her
fantasies by taking five different men in five days)

Connect with Red on Substance B

Substance B is a platform for independent authors to directly connect with their readers. Please visit Red's Substance B page where you can:

- Sign up for Red's newsletter
- Send a message to Red
- See all platforms where Red's books are sold

Visit Substance B today to learn more about your favorite independent authors.

CPSIA information can be obtained at www.ICGtesting.com
Printed in the USA
LVOW08s0025181016

509181LV00007B/56/P